KU-352-915

SUNNY DAYS

SUNNY DAYS

HELGA MORAY

Thorndike Press • Chivers Press
Thorndike, Maine USA Bath, England

This Large Print edition is published by Thorndike Press, USA and by Chivers Press, England.

Published in 1997 in the U.S. by arrangement with Robert Hale, Ltd.

Published in 1997 in the U.K. by arrangement with Robert Hale, Ltd.

U.S.   Hardcover   0-7862-1110-5   (Romance Series Edition)
U.S.   Hardcover   0-7540-3035-0   (Chivers Large Print)

Copyright © Helga Moray 1981

All rights reserved.

The text of this Large Print edition is unabridged.
Other aspects of the book may vary from the original edition.

Set in 16 pt. Plantin by Al Chase.

Printed in the United States on permanent paper.

British Library Cataloguing in Publication Data available

Library of Congress Cataloging in Publication Data

Moray, Helga.
    Sunny days / Helga Moray.
        p.   cm.
    ISBN 0-7862-1110-5 (lg. print : hc : alk. paper)
    1. Large type books. I. Title.
    [PR6025.O62S86 1997]
    823'.914—dc21   97-12334

'That you hope for nothing to last for ever, is the lesson of the revolving year and of the flight of time which snatches from us the sunny days.'

Horace, 65-8 B.C.

L. B. HOUNSLOW
LARGE PRINT COLLECTION

	SITE	DATE
1	DOM	11|97
2		
3		
4		
5		

One

The beautiful, blonde woman came into the crowded restaurant and stood for a moment in the entrance as she looked around. Then she saw the tall man leave a table and come toward her. Her trembling legs took her to meet him — he was the same! The same! Older of course and with grey in the dark hair.

"David — hello, I hope I haven't kept you waiting —"

"Only twenty-five years, Joan."

"That's a very complimentary remark."

Their greedy eyes searched each other's faces, oblivious of their surroundings. It was as if they alone existed out of all time. Then he became practical, grasped her elbow and walked her to the table and pulled her chair out. As she sat down he signalled to a hovering waiter to pour the champagne cooling in the silver bucket beside the table.

"Pink champagne!" she whispered. "You remembered."

"No trick to that — it was the only thing you liked to drink."

The same gruff, almost mocking voice that

years ago had often irritated her, even whilst its masculinity excited her.

Across the table his dark blue eyes stared at her with such intensity that their colour seemed to blacken around the pupils.

"By God you look wonderful, Joan — you've hardly changed."

"Oh, David." She smiled apologetically for the havoc of twenty-five years. "You've became a flatterer — but truthfully — *you've* changed very little."

He smiled and raised his glass to her and she silently toasted him, her green eyes large and wondering over the rim of her own glass as they drank to each other.

Ridiculous! Absurd! After a quarter of a century this man still affected her as he once had during their wild five year on-and-off affair in what was then glamorous Hollywood.

He replaced his glass on the table. "What extraordinary luck to have found you again, Joan."

Before she could answer the Maitre d' placed a long open menu before her then handed one to David. "Would you care to order, Doctor Murdoch?"

"Thank you." David glanced over the menu. "Ah there's blanquette de veau as a *plat du jour*. Would you like that, Joan?"

"Perfect and nothing to start with."

"Oh, but a little something — a Salad Nicoise, perhaps."

"A lovely choice." Had he suggested snake pie she would have agreed.

He swiftly ordered then told the Maitre d', "We'll carry on drinking champagne."

Left alone again he said, "There's so much I want to learn about you — I don't know where to begin asking questions. When did you come back from England? Have you been widowed a long time? When did you become a novelist? I also want to say that we were crazy fools to lose each other —"

"Miss Burke, please sign my autograph book. I was wild about your last novel." A woman was leaning over the table separating David from Joan.

'Go away! Go away!' she almost screamed.

"Grans! Grans, do wake up! I've brought your coffee!"

Joan moaned softly, twisting her head on the pillow. Sadly the meeting with David had only been a dream.

She sat up and took the small tray from her grand-daughter Karyn, wondering resentfully for what aeons of time was a heart condemned to agonise over an unfulfilled love?

"Grans! Were you having a nightmare?"

"Quite the contrary, darling. I was having a marvellous dream."

"What about, Grans?" Karyn went to draw the drapes and the New York sunshine flooded the room.

"Well," Joan gave a little laugh, "I was dreaming I was with an old beau — someone I once loved *very* much."

The eighteen-year-old Karyn looked amused at the idea. "What happened to him? Did he die?"

"No, he's a famous doctor in California." Joan started to pour her coffee. "We were very stupid, we quarrelled constantly and constantly made up again until we finally parted."

Karyn knew from old photos that Grans had been very beautiful. "Perhaps your dream might be prophetic; perhaps you're going to meet him again."

"In the dark I hope." Joan laughed shakily. "I wouldn't like the great David Murdoch to see what I look like aged fifty-four."

"You still look great so don't worry. Here, Grans, I've brought you my Graduation photo — came in the mail. Look!" Karyn held it up before Joan. "I'm disappointed, I look like a brunette not a blonde."

Joan took the photo to study it. "The photographer hasn't given enough light to your hair, but it's lovely really." The girl was a beauty with her heart-shaped face, softly smiling mouth, and wonderful eyes. So like herself at eighteen. "I'm glad he caught the spiritual look in your eyes."

"What Mother calls my 'vacant' look," Karyn laughed. "Too bad she didn't make it for the graduation."

"She tried everything to get back from London in time, but she couldn't because some idiot of an actor wouldn't sign his contract. Being a theatrical agent is no easy job you know."

"Oh, don't pity Mother, Grans, she loves her work — she's always with such glamorous men." Karyn slid her photograph onto a table. "Well, now that I've graduated from High School I want to go all out for ballet — after all Dad started me off when I was five — but Mother wants me to go to University. She can't afford it but she won't even hear of me trying ballet or T.V., or movies. Why is she so dead set against them?"

"Because she constantly sees what heartbreak trying to be an actress can bring."

"Not if you hit the top, Grans."

"Yes, darling, but for the one who *does* hit the top there are thousands who *don't*. You must have seen plenty of failures when you

11

lived in Hollywood when your Dad was alive."

"Ah — how different my life would have been if Dad hadn't shot himself." Karyn spoke the words slowly to give them full emphasis and it made Joan shudder to think how the unfortunate girl had almost been an eye-witness to the suicide. "You know, Grans, even though it's four years ago since that hellish night — sometimes it's as clear as if it's happening now." There was a tightening pain in her stomach that remembrance always brought.

"Don't dwell on it, Karyn, just pray for the repose of your father's soul."

"Oh I do — I do."

"He was such a wonderful man."

"He sure was, Grans. Did he do it because he was *really* wiped out?"

"I'm afraid so, his last two films were flops and God help him, his whole fortune was invested in them. It's lucky your mother had this New York apartment in her name when your lovely Beverly Hills home was sold to help pay off debts."

"I remember Pop rushing in and throwing his arms around Mother saying, 'Moira, honey — I've got it! I've really got the best film I've ever made!' Then the critics scorned it so much that he couldn't take it.

Poor, sweet Pop."

Karyn had recovered from the old familiar pain. "Well, I must move — Roy is picking me up soon." She made herself think of the golden-haired young giant who was the panacea to her tragic memories.

"He's still number one, is he?"

"Grans! How can you ask? He's been number one for over a year since he went up to Harvard Medical, but I'm upset because his parents want to whisk him off to Europe you know — the grand tour — all that jazz. He'll be gone *two months!*"

"But that's not so long, darling."

"It will be like eternity for me. I want him to refuse to go. After all there are five other kids in the family for the parents to gloat over and he doesn't *want* to leave me, he asked the parents to take me along but they turned that down."

"Perhaps they can't afford to take you."

"Grans! You must be kidding — you've forgotten Roy's surname. He's a *Van Buren.* He belongs to one of those old wealthy Dutch families, like the Stuyvesants, Roosevelts, Vanderbilts."

"Then why on earth don't they take you to Europe?"

"Because his mother thinks he's too young to be so keen on me. She wants to break us

13

up, but there's not a chance. Well — I must get into my jogging rig. We're meeting the gang in Central Park this morning. Go back to sleep, Grans; maybe you might dream of your Doctor Murdoch again."

A few minutes later, dressed in a jogging suit, Karyn dashed from the room into the hall and collided with her mother. With a forefinger Moira was massaging cream around her big brown eyes.

"What's the hurry, honey?"

"I'm going jogging with Roy in Central Park, then the gang's meeting for a barbecue at his place in Westchester."

From what seemed like her weight of thirty-six years Moira almost envied her daughter's young enthusiasm. "Sounds like fun, but don't get back too late. I'm dining out and I don't want to leave Grans alone too long."

"Okay! May I bring Roy in for supper with Grans? I'll fix it of course."

"Sure, sure, I want you to be happy."

"Thanks, Mother, I'll be seeing you."

Karyn ran to the hall door, unlocked the three locks, flung the door open and was out. Running to the elevator she heard her mother relocking the dead lock, double lock and chain lock.

Two

Karyn rushed out of the elevator across the hall to the wide entrance where Roy waited at the kerb in a red Porsche.

"Hi, sugar, late again." Roy's golden eyebrows drew together in a teasing frown as he leaned over to open the door for her. She slid in beside him. "Sorry, but Grans was telling me about an old love of hers and I had to listen." She swiftly pecked at his cheek as he eased the car into the traffic off Park Avenue.

"Sure you had to listen, Nugget."

Karyn loved his nickname for her, 'Nugget'. "Because you are as good as gold," he had told her soon after they had met.

"And I'm going to call you Viking," she had said. "I bet those brave sea-rovers looked like you." She had immediately been wild about his great height, strong bony face, his cap of thick gold hair and his eyes blue as the Pacific Ocean.

"Had a great hour with Dad this morning," Roy told Karyn. "He was on to this test-tube baby business. He's for it but somehow I'm not so sure if one should play around so much with nature. Of course who am I to argue against Dad; he's one of the greatest medical brains in the country."

"Sure you must stick to your own ideas, but I bet you're going to be just as fine a doctor as your father and your grandfather and great grandfather."

"This traffic is crazy for so early in June," exclaimed Roy as he turned the car into Fifth Avenue. "We're late already for the gang. Do you think you could miss your daily visit to St Patrick's?"

"Oh no please, Viking — I'll make it really snappy." She squeezed his arm. "I like to light a daily candle for Pop. He used to take me to Mass at St Patrick's so often when I was a kid."

Roy eased the car out of the traffic to pull up at the kerb before the great Cathedral.

"Okay, Nugget," he said. "Out you get, I'll circle the block."

As Karyn raced up the wide steps to the church Roy drove off thinking she was a fascinating mixture. Half of her seemed so vulnerable, needing protection, yet the other half was so God-damned independent. Her morals, too, were one for some book of Records, still a virgin at eighteen! Hardly believable with that beautiful body.

She had been at school with his sister Claudine, who was 'best-friend-mad' about her and when he had confided in Claudine about Karyn's refusal to make love, she had told him, "You're wasting your time and all your charisma on her, dear brother."

"But I'm hooked and I've never felt like this before."

"She's a virgin and is going to stay that way!"

"But why, for crikey's sake? She knows about the pill."

"Sure — sure."

"Then why is she holding out on me?"

"She's guarding her treasure for, 'the man I'll marry'."

"Well . . ." He felt somewhat mollified. "I guess that's not so crazy is it?"

"Damned right it's crazy. No man expects to take a virgin to the altar nowadays, but you can't change Karyn's Roman Catholic beliefs. Of course I adore her, have done for the four years I've known her, but I hate to see you wasting your time."

"Oh well — so what? She's great company. A guy isn't always screwing," he laughed, "there are times when his mind turns to other things."

Now driving back onto Fifth Avenue, Roy pulled up before the Cathedral steps and almost immediately Karyn came running down with her long blonde hair dancing on her shoulders.

"Wasn't that good timing?" she asked getting into the car.

"It sure was, Nugget, and how was God today?" asked Roy as he drove off.

"Fine as usual and sent you His best wishes." Some time ago she had decided flippancy was the best way to deal with Roy's irreligious attitude. "Tell me, Viking, don't you believe in God?"

"Oh yeah, though I don't go for the way he runs wars and permits diseases to flourish, but I leave religion to the oldsters. Of course Mother sometimes pays homage at St Thomas, because it's the Society church, I guess. But I don't get this thing about your old man. He was a Catholic, so how come he committed suicide? I reckoned your Church forbade it." He pulled up at a red light and glanced over at Karyn. "Okay my asking?"

She nodded. "Sure — that's bugged me for four years. In California the priest refused to bury Dad in consecrated ground because he was a suicide. But I believe that God has forgiven Dad — he must have had a mental blackout. You see that's why I never pass a church without lighting a candle and saying a prayer for the repose of his soul."

Roy leaned over and his big hand squeezed her tightly clasped hands in her lap. "Don't let it bug you, honey. I guess God welcomed your Dad over to His side. He musta been a helluva nice guy for you to be so mad about him."

Impatient motorists behind Roy started honking their horns so he inched the car forward as Karyn said, "He was wonderful! He took me everywhere with him and Mother, all over Europe."

"Maybe because you've travelled so much that you're different from other kids; maybe that's why I'm so hooked on you. Oh, talking of Europe — the news is bad. Mother is absolutely unmovable — I've got to go with the family!"

Disappointment weakened Karyn. "But you promised you'd say you don't *want* to go!" Why did he allow his mother to push him around? "She can't *make* you go — you're twenty-two!"

"Sure — sure, but there was a hulluva stink when I refused and Dad told me privately, 'Your mother's not well and it's very important for her to have the whole family together for this grand tour. She feels that after you've done your second year at Harvard, you can vacation on your own. You'd be helping me if you come willingly, son, after all, you're the eldest and should show a good example'." Roy shrugged his wide shoulders. "So what could I do Nugget?"

Disappointment and almost a fear of being parted from him fought with her fairmindedness for she supposed he must please his father. "It's just that I feel kinda lost at the idea of you being gone for two whole months."

"I'll miss *you* all right. What do you plan for the summer?"

"I dunno — go back to all-time ballet training, I guess, but something will turn up."

"But *not* on two legs in pants, I hope. You'll be a 'real' little Nugget whilst I'm gone, won't you — good as gold? Oh hell! Let's skip jogging today, let's pick up some steaks and beer and lam straight out to Westchester — I've got the key to the cottage. When we don't turn up at the Park the gang will jog without us and then come on to the cottage."

"Okay, that sounds fine."

Karyn was upset about his European trip and was glad to escape the gang for a while. He was feeling jumpy as hell — in a way quite new to him. What the hell was it? Jealousy at the idea of her without him but with loose bastards trying to screw her? Whilst for a year he had been wild to screw her himself, but had controlled himself. He couldn't talk of marriage — until he had his medical degree.

They hardly spoke again until they had left the city behind, bought the steaks and beer and were driving down a country lane. In the distance the stone cottage was embraced by clumps of flowering bushes and from not far off came the sound of the sea.

Roy pulled the car up before the cottage, jumped out, took the front steps two at a time, found the key in his pocket, unlocked the hall door, then went inside to throw the windows open. He looked around. Everything seemed okay. Dusty but who cared? He went back to the car, where Karyn was unloading the carton of food. "Give that to me, Nugget." He took it from her and she followed him into the house.

In the small kitchen as Roy put the provisions away, Karyn stared out of the window, across the green meadows sloping down to the sea. She was amazed and a little afraid at the way she was feeling. She did not want Roy to go to Europe and make love to someone over there. Perhaps she was a fool to hang onto her virginity — to keep refusing him when she loved him with all of her being. If she let him make love to her wouldn't that bind him to her during their separation? But it would be all wrong to lose her chastity!

He came up behind her, his hands on her shoulders, and she leaned back against him as she whispered words she had never said before. "Viking — I love you — I love you — it's awful that we must be separated for two months."

His hands slipped down to clasp her breasts, then he twisted her around to face him, holding her crushed up against him, "I love you too, Nugget, I'll think of you all the time I'm away but if you mean it that you *really* love me — *really* — then don't hold out against me. *Prove* that you love me."

"Half of me wants to — half of me says it's not right."

"But it *is* right for God's sake — we love each other. That's all that matters."

"Oh Viking!" She sank back into his arms and he scooped her up and carried her to the bedroom where he put her down on the double bed, then leaning over her he covered her face with kisses as his hands fumbled for the zipper on her jog-suit. He ripped it open then smiled down at her lovely body in tiny flowered bra and bikini. Then his excitement mounted uncontrollably.

"Nugget," he half grunted, "for God's sake, will you?"

"Yes," she whispered, "I will," and shut her eyes trying to blot out the guilty thoughts hammering at her as he ripped off his shorts, then pulled off her flowered bikini.

"Ah Nuggett . . . Nugget," he murmured as he climbed onto the bed and grasping her in his arms he threw a long leg over her as his hands under her buttocks roughly gathered her to him.

"Open your legs, honey for God's sake, — open them! Let me in!"

"Will it hurt, Viking?"

"No — no, I hope not." He started to push himself into her, but she cringed, contracting, so that he became mad with frustration. "Relax, honey, breathe through your mouth and relax — please — please."

She loved him, wanted to please him so separated her trembling legs and he pushed his hugeness into her making her body feel it would split. She cried out but his mouth covered hers, then he started to gyrate on her body and for a second she loathed it all, then a great surge of warmth starting inside

her, made her throb with unbelievable ec-
stasy and she clung to his shoulders as she
felt she was being lifted skywards with her
beloved Viking.

Three

She lay quite still beside him, his strong arm holding her against him. He was spread on his back still panting a little. Had she really done this thing? she asked herself. Deliberately sinned in her full consciousness? Oh dear God forgive me, she silently prayed with the guilty half of her mind whilst the other half rejoiced. It had been so marvellous! She and Viking had seemed joined as one body.

"Honey — was it okay for you?" he asked in a tender voice.

"Oh . . . it was wonderful. I can't even begin to try to explain it. Only I'm a little sad because now I'm not your Nugget — I'm no longer good as gold."

"You're even more my Nugget."

He leaned down and kissed her and their mouths clung to each other's until she pulled away and said, "But good-as-gold-girls don't sleep with men."

"You haven't, either — you and I have made love together — that's something quite different." His hand fondled her breast. "Darling, let's go off somewhere for a week on our own before I leave. Can you cook up an excuse to give your family?"

"Oh how lovely — a whole week alone together, yes I'll invent some kind of excuse."

"But, sugar, first you gotta get the pill. We don't want any accidents."

"Oh — yes, of course — I'll go to the Clinic where all my friends go." She sat up. "Hey — listen! Cars are coming! It's the gang."

They jumped up, dragging on their shorts and jog-suits.

"I'll hold them off, honey, whilst you do the bed." Roy raced to the living-room to put on a cassette and by the time the two cars pulled up, Karyn was in the kitchen taking steaks from the fridge.

As everyone started pouring into the house she called out, "Hi, I'm just fixing lunch." She went into the living-room to greet them.

Dark-haired Claudine Van Buren smiled at Karyn knowingly. "How come you two didn't make it to the Park?"

"We got a late start so decided to come straight out here. Roy brought loads of steaks, as we were expecting you to roll up."

"Great! I'm starved, it's crazy for me to jog to take weight off. It gives me such an appetite I eat the pounds back on again."

"Me too." Lynda Dawson giggled. She

was a tall, long-legged red head, who had been a school fellow of Karyn's and Claudine's.

For some months now Lynda's boyfriend had been Roy's brother Nicholas. Though a year Roy's junior, he and Roy could almost pass for twins.

The sixth member of the gang was twenty-two year old Carl Brand, Roy's closest friend since childhood and his room-mate at Harvard. Carl was also reading medicine. He was dark, heavily built and like Roy and Nicholas, a fine athlete. Months ago he had first climbed into Claudine's bed and was now hooked on her. His family enjoyed long established wealth.

"Okay, you guys," Roy yelled over the blaring music. "Let's get the barbecue going — whilst the girls season the steak and make the salads."

With their cans of beer the men moved on to the little patio. "God, what a great day!" Nicholas lifted his face to the sun. "I'd like to stay out here all week."

"Not a chance, man," Roy laughed, "Mother has us lined up for the next few days to take God knows what kind of shots against the diseases she imagines we'll pick up in Europe."

Carl laughed dryly. "So your mother won

over Karyn eh? I thought she would."

"Well, if Karyn were my girl I'm damned if I'd leave her," Nicky said quietly. "It's not only that she's so God darned beautiful, there's something — I dunno what it is — but something special about her. Of course, according to Claudine, she's the world's number one virgin, so I guess it's safe to leave her."

"For Christ sake!" Roy burst out, "I don't give a damn how much we three discuss dames — but Hell. Karyn's different!"

"Sorry man — sorry." Nicky exchanged a knowing look with Carl.

Karyn came out carrying a wooden platter with the steaks, and took them to Roy. With a long fork he placed them on the barbecue.

"Why don't you lazy louts bring knives and forks out and set the table?" Roy asked Nicky and Carl.

Nicky got up to go to the kitchen to help the other girls.

"I suppose I'd better lend a hand too," Carl grinned meaningly at Roy, "I can see barbecuing steaks is a job only for two."

"Get out of here, you louse, and leave honest people to their labours." Roy gave him a wink then turning to Karyn said, "Nicky reckons I'm crazy to leave you, Nugget."

"I agree with him."

He stared down deep into her eyes. "But I can trust you can't I, darling? . . . I'm safe with you?"

She closed her eyes, then opened them as if making a vow, "You bet you're — safe — I'm only yours, Viking."

After lunch of steaks, salad, apple pie, washed down with beer, Nicky lit a cigarette, then passed it around for everyone to have a pull.

When it came to Karyn, she said, "You know I don't smoke."

"Oh, come on, Karyn — break down and have a pull," Claudine coaxed. "It will make you feel on top of the world."

"No thanks, the thought of pot scares me."

"Oh, honey-chile, you're too damned pure to live," Lynda snapped.

Karyn suddenly flushed with shame for now her morals were almost as loose as Lynda's and Claudine's, both of whom she had secretly disapproved of for all the men they had slept with.

As if he sensed something of Karyn's dismay Roy said, "Let's cool it, shall we, if Karyn disapproves of pot — well it's a free country. She has a right to her beliefs."

"Sure, sure — it's Karyn's life." Claudine

29

took several more drags on the cigarette, then put it between Carl's lips. "Get with it, lover boy," she whispered, "then let's head for the beach — to our favourite spot."

A few minutes later they had all gone, leaving Roy and Karyn alone in the cottage.

The sun was beginning to sink when they left the bed, with Karyn feeling lightheaded from lovemaking. "My bones seem turned to jelly, Viking, I'm almost too tired to dress."

"I'll help you," he said and dressed her as if she were a beloved child.

"Viking darling, you're wonderful to me."

"I love you — I love you, Nugget." His big hands cupped her face as he leaned down to kiss her. "I know what you did today wasn't easy — I mean ditching your beliefs — but don't worry, darling, I'll never forget it — and I'll never let you regret it."

Her arms went up around his neck. "Darling Viking. When I'm with you I feel safe — as if nothing could ever harm me — but come on, darling, we'd better clean up the patio. We can't leave all that mess for the warden's wife."

"Right. I'll tackle the outside — whilst you straighten up in here." He strode out of the room.

The cottage was tidy, the dishes rinsed, by the time the others returned looking tousled, sleepy and contented.

"Too much sun," Nicky said defensively, "Lynda and I fell asleep. Any beer going?" He went into the kitchen.

Claudine yawned. "How about you, Karyn? Did Roy entertain you reading from a medical book?"

Then she stopped to stare at Karyn, for there was a new glow about her much loved friend. Karyn's huge eyes seemed feverishly shiny, her beautiful lips were swollen. Wowie — at last! Claudine silently cheered; Karyn had jumped off the pedestal. Good for her. Claudine's look went to Roy; a light seemed to be shining from within him too. Bully for Roy, bully for Karyn. They had obviously made wonderful music together. It was easy for Claudine to see their lovemaking had been something special.

"Why the hell, Claudine, are you looking at me like a mother hen at a favourite chick?" Roy brought his golden eyebrows together in a frown.

She shot him a tender smile, and Roy sensed that Claudine, with her animal-like instinct, guessed that he and Karyn had become lovers.

Driving back to town, Roy told Karyn.

31

"I've a hunch Claudine has tumbled to us."

"But how ever could she?"

"Oh, I guess it's written all over our faces. Being in love like we are is rather like people carrying banners with big printed announcements on them."

A joyous laugh tinkled out of her as she laid her head on his shoulder. "Well I *feel* so happy I just hope grandmother won't notice."

"You think she expected you to stay a virgin at eighteen?"

"I guess so. She married at eighteen and so did my mother. I told you this morning about Grans' romantic dream of an old love of hers. She was quite excited about it. Can you imagine at fifty-four?"

"Sure, why not? The sex urge lasts a long time, you know, lots of women in their fifties are damned randy."

"Oh, not Grans, for heaven's sake!" Karyn felt quite shocked. "But she *was* rather cute about this Doctor David Murdoch — she says he's famous now . . ."

"I'll say he is!"

"Darling, do you know him?"

"I sure do; he's one of Dad's close friends. Dad was on the 'phone to him last night in California. He's arriving here next week."

"Oh no! That's too extraordinary! Is he nice?"

"A swell guy. Last time I saw him he was trying to persuade me to specialize in his line of medicine. He's a woman specialist."

"I see. Will you stay for supper tonight with Grans and me?"

"I can't honey — I'm sorry but Mother's planned to tell us about our European itinerary this evening." He gave an indulgent laugh. "She's going to give us a potted culture course."

Damn his possessive mother! Did she expect to always have Roy under her delicate thumb? "Well, at least come in for a few minutes and tell Grans about Doc Murdoch."

"Sure, honey, I'll see you in."

When they arrived at the apartment house entrance they met Karyn's mother and a young flashily good-looking, dark man on the way out.

To Roy, Moira seemed to be a swirl of shiny dark hair, glistening eyes, whiter-than-white teeth. Her beauty and youthfulness always surprised him.

"Too bad we are just on the wing," Moira said. "Oh this is Cervantes Castillo." She indicated the tall man beside her. "We're going to Jake Rhine's party — every film producer in the business will be there. One of them is bound to see that Cervantes is star material." Smiling at Roy and Karyn she grasped her client's arm and swept out with him.

Karyn looked at Roy and shrugged as they moved toward the elevator. "Mother tries *not* to introduce me to her young beaux — having an eighteen-year-old daughter she thinks is bad for her youth image."

Upstairs they found Joan seated before the T.V. in the living-room. It was a spacious room furnished in excellent taste with English antiques. Joan turned the T.V. off as they entered.

"How nice to see you, Roy — do sit down."

"I'm afraid I can't stay, Mrs Clements."

"Roy just came up to tell you about Doc Murdoch, Grans."

Joan's eyes stretched wide in surprise whilst her heart banged so absurdly, she had to wait a second before she asked, "Do you know him Roy?"

"Yeah, he's a great friend of Dad's."

"What an extraordinary coincidence!" Is he still married? she longed to ask. Has he any children? Instead she said, "Is he still practising in Beverly Hills?"

"And how! He runs one of the finest

women's clinics in the country. He'll be here next week. Would you like me to give him a message?"

"Well — no — I don't think so thank you, Roy. You see our friendship was so long ago, he might almost have forgotten all about it."

"I'll bet he hasn't," Roy said politely. "Well now I guess I have to go."

Karyn saw him to the door where they kissed swiftly but passionately. "I'll call you later, honey," Roy murmured as his arms released her and he reluctantly left. Now that at last they were lovers he felt he could never have enough of her.

Four

Jake Rhine's penthouse on 70th and Park was so crowded that new arrivals had to almost push their way in between the closely packed bodies.

"Lord what a crush," Moira muttered to Cervantes as she took the glass of champagne he had plucked from a butler's tray.

"It's great to be here, Moira." He gulped greedily at his champagne.

"Yeah," she nodded as her eyes swept over the throng. Producers, money men, actors, actresses, many famous faces of yesteryear and plenty of new young beauties, ready to strip for the chance of a walk-on part. Writers tried to look intellectual, to stand out from the herd that lived by their looks, but loving the smell of money, for Jake Rhine was a millionaire who spent like one. The Press was here in force, picking up gossip, inventing it if none were available.

Moira hated the whole scene but sharply warned herself, 'I eat and pay my bills through contact with these people.'

Suddenly she felt a sloppy kiss on her bare shoulder and indignantly swung around to confront a heavily built, middle-aged man. "Hi, gorgeous!"

"Why, Ben Locke! I haven't seen you for years." Once a foremost film producer after three bad films he had slipped. "Wherever have you been hiding, Ben?"

"I've been all over the world, baby — making pictures."

She swiftly recalled some vague rumours and tried to cover her *faux pas* — Ben might be helpful to Cervantes. "Of course, you were in Mexico City!" Then she laid on the flattery, "establishing their film industry. Meet my newest client — of Spanish extraction, Cervantes Castillo."

"Glad to know you, Mr Locke." Cervantes flashed his wide smile. Meant to hit Ben between the eyes with Cervantes film-star potential.

Client or lover? Ben wondered as he shook Cervantes' hand. "So you're Moira's client, eh. Maybe I can use you in my new film." He turned to Moira, "That interest you, sugar?"

"Oh yes, Ben."

"Right!" He would show her he was still a big shot. "Okay. Ring my secretary in the morning, I'm at the St Regis. She'll arrange a test for Cervantes at the Long Island studio."

"Great, Ben! Who are you making the film for?" Moira asked.

"I've got Mexican backing — unlimited." He put his mouth to her ear muttering, "It's from a drug syndicate that owns thousands of acres, growing marijuana in the interior of Mexico. But so what? If *I* don't help use their filthy money, some other guy *will*." Determined to impress her he went on. "I've got a real sweet deal, baby, it will put me back on top of the heap again." He caught at Cervantes' arm, "I gotta have Latin artists who speak Spanish and English. I want to shoot in both languages at the same time."

"I speak both languages, Mr Locke."

"He's absolutely fluent in English and Spanish," Moira assured Ben who was snapping his fingers at a Press photographer.

When the man came over Ben said, "I'll give you a break, kid — get a load of Cervantes Castillo — a Spanish star! Hey get into the line-up, Moira."

The three of them arms around each other stood for the photographer and Ben went on, "Just caption it, 'Seen at Jake Rhine's fabulous party — Cervantes Castillo, the Spanish star, with Ben Locke, who is producing films in Mexico City, and Moira Kirbo, Mr Castillo's agent'."

"Thanks a lot, Mr Locke." The photographer jotted the names down. "Hey, Baryshnikov's just arrived — I gotta get him."

People's excited murmurs started to overlap each other's.

"Hey, Moira!" Ben grasped her arm. "It's getting too bloody hot here, let's blow the joint. What do you say to dinner at Sardi's?"

"Well, fine, although I really wanted to see a couple of people here — but another time will do." Wise to stick to Ben, he might give Cervantes a contract if the Test pleased him.

In the living-room Karyn and Joan sat eating from trays.

"You make a delicious jam omelette, darling," Joan said.

"Thanks, Grans. You taught *me* but how come you never taught Mom to cook?"

"But, darling, until she was nine, we lived in Bel Air with a staff of six."

"Grandfather was really rich, wasn't he?"

"Yes, he was one of the top producers in Hollywood. When he proposed to me in London I jokingly said, 'Yes, I'd love to marry you, but I want to go round the world on my honeymoon.' 'Okay,' he said, 'I'll take you on my yacht'."

"Phew — Grans — sounds like a dream — doesn't it?"

Joan visualized her first husband, Brian Henekey, with hazel twinkling eyes and untidy curly brown hair. "Yes, it *was* like a dream, we sailed for fourteen months on our honeymoon. It *was* all fantastic, until I was pregnant and so miserably seasick that I was glad to get back to our lovely home in Bel Air."

"Grandpa must have loved you so much, *why* did you leave him? I've never dared ask before. Is it okay now?"

Joan had dreaded this question. "Of course, darling. I suppose I had been too spoiled and grew selfish so that I couldn't endure any unpleasantness. You see, your grandfather was a very heavy drinker and I hated that. Then the big difference in our ages bothered me."

"Yeah, I guess the generation gap was too big, but life was okay again for you when you married Basil. He was a great guy. I used to love our visits to you in England, they . . ." She broke off as the telephone rang. "That must be Roy for me."

She raced to the kitchen to speak in private and grabbed the telephone.

"Hi, Nugget."

"Oh — hi!" She was so excited, her breath

came short. "I thought you'd never call, Viking."

"Sorry, couldn't get to the 'phone sooner — had to watch all the coloured slides mother had lined up. She wants us to be acquainted with the statuary and other wonders we're going to visit."

"Not a bad idea." She must try not to be a drag about his trip. "Was the whole family there?"

"Sure — all of us, but my kid sister of five has been sent to bed. What have you been up to honey?"

"Listening to Grans. She fascinates me with bits about her honeymoon. She sailed in Grand-dad's yacht for fourteen months, visiting fifty-six countries."

"No kidding! That was some honeymoon! People aren't so lucky nowadays, Nugget." His voice dropped to a whisper. "We started a sort of honeymoon of our own today, right?"

"Uh-ha, yes — it was so wonderful." She shut her eyes visualizing lying on the bed with him. "Just wonderful."

"Wish we were back there, Nugget, this minute — wish — wish — wish."

"Me too — darling, I love you so much, Viking."

"And I love you, my Nugget. Say, I can't

see you first thing tomorrow, Dad's offered
to let me make rounds with him at the clinic
so I'll pick you up at five o'clock at your
place. Okay by you?"

"Sure, sure!"

"Okay, hon, I gotta go now, my crazy
brother Nicky is calling me back to the library. I love you — love you."

"I love you, Viking, and I'm going to bed
to dream about today — and us —"

"Yeah, me too — darling — darling."

The telephone clicked; Viking was gone.
Karyn felt quite breathless, light-headed, as
if she'd been running non-stop. Crazy to feel
like this about Viking after she'd been dating
him for so long, but what had happened
between them today seemed to have welded
them together as one person. She felt she
was a part of that big, laughing golden boy-
man.

Five

Roy tried to slip quietly back into the spacious library. The family still sat as he had left them, his youngest sister had been sent to bed and his sisters, Cynthia and Robin, played dominoes in a corner, Claudine sitting near Nicky and their dark-haired, stockily built father; their golden-haired, pale-faced mother wrapped in delicate beige chiffon draperies, reclined on a sofa, as always she exuded an impression of old world aristocratic fragility.

"Ah, you're back, Roy." Ann Van Buren spoke languidly. "Where on earth did you go?" She allowed a tinge of reproach to sound in her voice. "You slipped off so mysteriously."

"But I only went to 'phone, Mother."

"It must have been very important to pull you away from our nice little 'family' conference."

"Oh, I'll bet it was important," Claudine laughed teasingly. "He 'phoned Karyn."

"Karyn?" Ann raised her eyebrows as she asked with assumed ignorance, "Who is this Karyn?"

43

"She's a school friend of mine," Claudine said, "the girl we wanted to come on the trip with us but you said, 'No'. Surely you remember about her, the one whose father committed suicide — almost in front of her —"

Furious, Roy burst out, "Can't you find any other way to identify Karyn, for God's sake!"

"Really, Roy, do control your temper," Ann said in her coldest English voice. "Poor girl, she must be so psychologically disturbed after such a tragedy — almost deranged."

"You couldn't be more wrong, Mother!" Roy spoke in quiet anger. "Karyn's one of the sanest people I know."

Ann's cat grey eyes played over his handsome face as her heartbeat quickened. Did he think he was in love with this chit? "Well, my dear Roy, you don't have to be so vehement in her defence."

"This is all becoming rather stupid, isn't it?" Doctor Van Buren said. "Roy naturally objects to the supposition that a friend of his is psychologically disturbed."

"Dad, *I* didn't say she was!" Claudine defended herself. "It was Mother who thought Karyn might have a trauma on account of the suicide."

"Karyn's a marvellous person," Nicky defensively burst out, hoping to take some of the heat off Roy so that their mother would not guess he was in love with Karyn and so get a down on her. "Karyn's as normal as any of us here," he added.

"I can vouch for that too," Claudine nodded.

"Oh, I'm so glad." Ann's voice was clear, cool, like a ping on Waterford crystal. "Her mother is a theatrical agent, I believe, isn't she?" Her delicate nostrils drew together as if to avoid an offensive odour.

"Yes," Roy snapped, "and her grandmother's a novelist."

"Ah yes, she writes historical romances, doesn't she? Even butchers stock those paperbacks." Ann gave a tinkling laugh, "they're sold by the yard, I believe."

Roy and Nicky exchanged a familiar look that said, 'The bitch is on the warpath' then Roy said, "Well, now that you've so kindly disposed of Karyn and her family, what's next on the Agenda or should I say 'who's' next?"

"Really, Roy, you are being most disrespectful to me."

"I didn't mean any disrespect, Mother." Roy gave her a forced grin. "Shall we get on with our educational programme? It's almost eleven o'clock."

"No, I've been too upset," Ann gathered her full draperies about her and stood up; her husband and children immediately rose with her. "I don't feel too well, I'd better go to bed."

Doctor Van Buren put his cognac down and went to offer his arm to his wife. "I'll see you up, dear, and safely tucked into bed." He shot an appealing glance at Roy who understanding the unspoken request to make peace went to kiss his mother's cool cheek.

"Now take care of yourself, Mother," he said. "We want you well and strong when we go careering around Europe."

Mollified, Ann caught at her adored son's hand. "Thank you, my darling, I can't wait for our trip." Then she held her cheek up for Nicky to kiss. She smiled at him, patted his face, her wonderful golden-haired sons were part of her very heartbeat. Leaning on Peter Van Buren's arm she moved to the door which Nicky sprang to open for her.

When their parents had gone the younger girls went off to bed, and Nicky poured out three brandies for Roy, Claudine and himself.

"Oh Lord, Roy — I must have been crazy to have said that about Karyn and the 'phone," Claudine said miserably, "but I honestly didn't think Mother would spring onto her English high horse about Karyn."

"But hell — you know damn well that any girl Nicky or I take a shine to Mother turns thumbs down on." Roy gulped down some cognac.

Claudine pulled a grimace, "Yeah, she's so crazy about her 'tall handsome sons' that it makes my stomach flip over. It beats me that Dad isn't jealous of you two."

"That's crazy talk," Nicky muttered but he uncomfortably knew there was too much of the Oedipus shadow about their mother's love for Roy and himself.

"I wonder if she really feels sick or is it all part of her Ophelia act?" Roy asked.

Close as she was to her brothers Claudine still did not tell them how much she despised their mother. "Who knows how sick she is? But you must have noticed she falls sick every time she wants her own way."

"Yeah, poor old Dad," said Nicky. "She's been pulling her delicate health on him for years."

"But for God's sake, man, Dad's just gotta know it's psychological," Roy said. "She can't fool a Doctor like him. Well, I'm going to hit the sack. No percentage in discussing Mother, she's got us stymied."

"Yeah, let's have a smoke to forget our

heebie-jeebies, but not down here. If Dad comes back he'll smell pot," Claudine warned. "Let's go to your den."

Nicky and Roy's bedrooms were separated by their den and now Claudine and Nicky sat there on a couch sharing a cigarette. Roy had gone to bed to think of Nugget.

Nicky and Claudine spoke in low voices. They had both guessed that at last Roy and Karyn had become lovers and now they told each other how glad they were about it. Then Claudine said, "Roy's going to have a tough time with Mother. She already has her daggers into Karyn. Oh Lord I wish she were a different kind of woman." She pulled on the cigarette inhaling deeply.

"What bugs me is why Dad ever married Mother," said Nicky. "Oh I know she was an Earl's grand-daughter and a great beauty but couldn't he tell that she was a cold fish? And in her aristocratic English way I bet she never thought he was good enough for her, even though he was the scion of the wealthy Van Buren family."

"You're right, Nicky. I am sure she never loved *him,* only his millions and all the jewels he showered on her. Poor old Pop, he should find himself a nice cosy little mistress." Claudine held up the cigarette stub. "All gone — time for shut-eye."

She stood up, picked up her shoes, pecked Nicky on the cheek and padded down the deeply carpeted corridor to her own suite.

Six

"Isn't it great that Carl has got his folks' cabin in the Adirondacks for us?" said Karyn two nights later as she sat with Roy in an all-night drug store.

She smiled up into his delighted looking face, "It's wonderful! I just can't wait to go. I'm sure I'll be okay telling Grans and Mother that I'm going to stay with Lynda and her father. I hate the lies, but what else can I do? But, Viking, I still can't get over your mother inviting me for dinner at the end of the week?"

"Yeah, she certainly surprised me when she said, 'Darling, ask your friend Karyn to dine. I'd like to get to know her.' "

"But you always said she turned like an iceberg at the mention of you and any girl."

"You can say that again, and the same with Nicky." He lit a cigarette and slowly exhaled. Through half-closed eyes he watched the smoke drifting off, then said, "I don't get it — I think she's up to some trick but I can't figure out what it is."

"Maybe not, Viking — maybe she's just trying to please you."

"Yeah, maybe," he murmured. "Anyhow, there's nothing she can do to alter my love for you — you know that."

She smiled into his eyes and nodded, thinking, but she's taking you away from me for two whole months.

"Well, at last they've invited you," Moira burst out indignantly, "and about time too! This will be the first time you've been to the Van Burens' great white mansion — isn't that so?"

"No, I've been with Claudine several times but only to her bedroom and living-room. But I don't know what to wear — my graduation dress is kid-stuff."

Moira was excitedly contemplating the idea of Karyn married someday to Roy.

"Yes, your graduation dress won't do," she agreed. "Let's see what I have that might suit you."

In Moira's bedroom, they stood before the long open closet, carefully going through twenty or more beautiful gowns. Karyn chose a pale lime jersey, with clinging lines and a slit up the front.

"This one! Could I borrow this, Mother?"

"Okay — try it on, but maybe it's a bit too sophisticated for you."

The silk jersey clung to Karyn's slim body

like another skin, the low plunge neckline discreetly showed the swelling of her lovely breasts and the slit in the skirt parted to frame her legs. Moira, whose own legs were good, thought Karyn's the most sensational she had ever seen.

"Yeah — it's super on you," Moira said, "colour, style, just perfect. Now what about your hair? Up maybe?"

"No. Roy loves it hanging long, on my shoulders. Oh *thanks* a million, Mother, for the dress." Karyn planted a kiss on Moira's cheek. "I'll be super careful of it."

"Okay, honey — hope you have a great time. I've got to change now — I'm dining with two gays who want to read their latest play to me."

"Right, I'm off." Karyn dashed out and into the living room calling, "How do I look, Grans?"

Joan gazed at her with wide, delighted eyes. "Like a picture — just beautiful! The colour is so becoming to your slight tan and your hair — it also makes your eyes look greener."

"Oh thanks, Grans. I just hope I wow Roy's parents. Well, I must dash and get ready."

Karyn left the cab, rang a bell next to the

tall wrought-iron gates that pierced the high wall surrounding the great white mansion, then a footman admitted her into a marble paved courtyard banked all around with masses of azalea bushes.

The courtyard led to a wide corridor, richly carpeted in cream, the walls hung with large, sombre portraits of past Van Burens. The footman stopped before large double doors and with a fastly beating heart Karyn followed the man into the room as he announced, "Miss Karyn Kirbo."

A dozen or so people were sitting and standing in the magnificent drawing-room, chatting and drinking champagne. Then Claudine hurried forward with a wide smile.

"Hi, Karyn," she said in a loud welcoming voice; then swiftly murmured, "Mother's so madly jealous of Roy and Nick that we arranged for me to meet you and put her off the scent a bit." Then, again in a loud voice, "You look gorgeous! Absolutely gor . . . ge . . . ous!"

Though nervous by what Claudine had whispered, Karyn forced a smile and said, "You look great too."

"Thanks — well come and meet the dragon."

Mrs Van Buren stood near a drum table, leaning delicate fingers on it as though needing slight support. She was talking to a smartly gowned, bejewelled woman and appeared unconscious of Karyn and Claudine's approach.

"Mother, this is Karyn," Claudine said cheerily.

Ann Van Buren turned slowly, her strange cat-like grey eyes unsmiling. "How do you do? You're just as lovely as Claudine said you were." The woman beside Ann drifted off and Peter Van Buren replaced her. "This is my husband," Ann said, "Doctor Peter Van Buren — my dear this is Karyn Kirbo."

"Delighted to know you, Karyn." Peter held out a strong square hand and as Karyn put her cold fingers into his warm clasp, her fears of Mrs Van Buren were eased.

"It's very kind of you to have invited me tonight Mrs Van Buren," Karen said, feeling terribly ill at ease under Ann's deliberate cold scrutiny.

"But it's our pleasure, Karyn," Doctor Van Buren swiftly said.

"Yes, indeed," Ann almost cooed as Roy joined them. "Roy darling, you were very remiss in your praise of Karyn. You never told us she was such an outstanding beauty."

Roy flushed uncomfortably. "Well, that shows how dumb I am, doesn't it?" He shot Karyn a swift intimate look, but he was wary of his mother, for he didn't trust her an inch.

"You bear no resemblance to your mother Karyn, do you?" Ann said, and looking down on the drumtable picked up a newspaper carefully folded to a three column photograph. "I saw this a couple of days ago — so I know there is no resemblance." She handed Karyn the newspaper.

As Karyn glanced at the photograph, Dr Van Buren, Roy and Claudine looked at it over her shoulder and Karyn felt a pain attack her low in the stomach. Her mother wearing a far too plunging neckline was smiling exaggeratedly as she stood between the flashy looking actor, Cervantes, and a common brawny man. They all had their arms around each other. The caption blurred for Karyn but she saw enough to know the photograph had been taken at Jake Rhine's penthouse party and the common man was Ben Locke. It was tawdry and cheap-looking and Karyn felt ashamed. She kept her face lowered over the paper.

"Well, well," Doctor Van Buren said with forced cheerfulness, "my wife is right Karyn, you and your mother are not alike at all."

Roy silently took the paper out of Karyn's hand and said, "Come on and meet everyone." He grasped her elbow and steered her away.

He felt like a killer in his heart — his mother was a cruel bitch but now she was out in the open. She had cleverly demonstrated to his father that Karyn's theatrical background did not belong with the Van Burens. She had invited Karen so that she might demolish her, but to hell with the bitch — Karyn was his love and nothing was going to interfere with that. He felt her arm trembling under his hand and he murmured, "Sorry about that, darling — but forget it, will you?" He took two glasses of champagne from a passing butler and gave one to Karyn.

"I am not ashamed of my mother, Viking." The words burst from Karyn. "In fact I'm proud of her but that damned photo is horrible."

"Who cares, sweetheart? It's not important to us."

"But it is to your parents. That's why your mother staged the little scene. It's crazy isn't it that she is trying to wipe me out with you when she really doesn't know anything about me."

"Hi, Karyn!" Nicky joined them. "Wowie, aren't you the original all-time, beautiful golden girl!"

"Thanks, Nicky." The admiration in his blue eyes was comforting. "But I don't feel so hot."

"How come?"

Roy swiftly told him what had happened and with tightening jaw muscles he added, "I might punish the bitch by dropping out of her Van Buren Circus to Europe."

"Christ man! No one could blame you."

"No, no Viking — don't be vengeful that wouldn't make her like me; she'd hate me all the more."

"Who on earth could ever hate anyone who looks like you?" A tall sun-tanned man, dark hair streaked with grey, stood looking down with approval on Karyn. "Hi, Roy, Nicky, what must a man do to get an introduction? Surely you are not apprehensive of an old boy like me."

"Sorry about that," Roy grinned. "Doctor David Murdoch this is Karyn Kirbo."

"Oh . . . oo," Karyn cooed, "it's *you!*"

"Lovely girl — I must be going crazy but I'd swear we've never met."

"No — no, *we* haven't but I've heard about you from my grandmother."

"Is that right? And who is she?"

"She's a novelist, writes under the name of Joan Burke."

His deep blue eyes almost closed as he

said, "Yes, I know of her." He wanted to be sure it was the woman whose face and voice had plagued him for so many years. "What's her married name?"

"Clements."

No, that wasn't her, sombrely he shook his head. "Don't know a Mrs Clements."

"Ah! But, I've just thought of something. You might have known her by her *first* married name — Joan Henekey — my grandfather was Brian Henekey."

He stared at Karyn as he said, "Good God! You mean to tell me that you are Joan's grand-daughter? You know you resemble her. How is she?"

"Just fine, we live quite near here on Park Avenue. Grans is a widow — and so is my mother and . . ."

"Dinner is served!" the butler intoned, and people started to put their champagne glasses down and to move toward the double doors. Karyn was glad to have Doctor Murdoch with her and Roy and Nicky although she had recovered from her brush with Ann Van Buren.

In the large dining-room the long mahogany table was beautiful with Venetian lace runners, baccarat goblets and Georgian silver tableware and candelabra. A map of the table and seating cards in crystal holders carried the names of the eighteen diners.

To her dismay Karyn saw she was divided from Mrs Van Buren by only one seat. Thank God the person was Doctor Murdoch, who was on Ann's immediate right. Mean of Mrs Van Buren to put her at the other end of the table from Roy.

Amongst light chatter everyone was seated and as the footmen started to serve lobster thermidor, Karyn turned to Carl who was her other dinner partner. She was relieved to have a friend near her, but before they could start to talk, Ann leaned across Doctor Murdoch and addressed Karyn.

"And what are you doing with yourself this summer, Karyn?"

"Well I'm not quite sure yet, my family hasn't made any definite plans, Mrs Van Buren."

"You're not planning a trip to Europe are you, to meet up with Roy?"

Indignation sent the blood flying to Karyn's face, "Most certainly not!"

"Really? I had an idea that you might follow him but perhaps my instinct is deserting me." A laugh tinkled out of Mrs Van Buren's pale lips as she told Doctor Murdoch, "You know my instinct has always been most remarkable — I see through subterfuge and deceit. I'd like everyone to believe that."

He could not see why she gave the subject such importance, but he said lightly, "Sounds as if you have extra-sensory perception."

"But I do — how clever of you to realize that. I know just as well as I'm talking to you now that my eldest son, Roy, will some day be President of the United States!" Her deep set grey eyes were burning defiantly at Karyn.

"I didn't know Roy was interested in politics. I thought he was mad on medical research," Karyn said.

"That's his whim at the moment but both my sons lean on me for advice. They'd never do anything against my wishes and are well aware that *I* know what's best for them — and Roy has been chosen by Fate to be President — *nothing*, no unsuitable marriage or anything else will be allowed to stand in his way." Mrs Van Buren smiled triumphantly as she toyed with her lobster. "First of course he'll get his medical degree from Harvard — then into politics he goes! Women will of course pursue him, that's natural for he has the looks of a God as well as the Van Buren millions, but I shall protect him from these women — I warn you!"

"But why talk like that to me," Karyn

flared. "I haven't . . ."

"Mrs Van Buren," Murdoch interrupted, "what's more important is how you are feeling yourself. Peter was telling me that you're not very well." Christ! The woman was a psycho — she had worked herself up into almost a maniacal fit of jealousy over Roy and this poor girl.

Suddenly Ann started to breathe in short gasps. "I'm ill . . . ill . . . nobody understands . . . they all upset me."

Murdoch sprang from his chair to help her as she attempted to rise, then her husband rushed up and the two men, arms supporting Ann, managed to walk her from the room. There was a commotion around the table but Nicky called out, "Don't worry, everyone — this is not serious — please go on with dinner!" Seated beside Karyn, Carl squeezed her arm. "Poor kid, the mad bitch really laid into you."

"She's horrible — horrible Carl."

"She guesses Roy is in love with you and she's going all out to stop it."

At that moment Roy came to sit in Murdoch's place beside Karyn, "Christ! I'm sorry, darling," he murmured. "I heard bits of her tirade from where I was sitting, I should have warned you that sometimes she seems off her rocker."

61

Karyn was trembling from the shock of his mother's attack but she said, "It's okay, Viking — but I didn't know she could be like that — poor you."

"It's okay, we're used to her. Now let's eat in peace, she won't be back tonight; she thinks she's accomplished her plan of scaring you off." He squeezed her hands held clenched in her lap. "But I love you, Nugget," he murmured, "that's all that counts."

Karyn nodded, then tremblingly picked up a fork to spear some lobster. It fell off the prongs, making a big greasy mark on her mother's $500 dress, but Karyn was too upset to care about it.

Seven

David Murdoch, and Doctor Peter Van Buren, sat in a secluded corner of the smoking room in the Harvard Club. Each man held a bourbon on the rocks in his hand, as Murdoch spoke in a low voice.

"I gave Ann a complete examination at your Clinic today, Peter, then I studied the reports on her tests and X-rays so now I can assure you that physically there is absolutely nothing wrong with her." He hesitated, embarrassed to say what must hurt his old friend. "Her 'sickness' is entirely imaginary, Peter — all in her mind."

Frowning, Van Buren sipped his drink. "You've confirmed my suspicions but I've been loath to give them credence."

"That's understandable, Peter, but now you must accept the unpleasant truth — Ann is more than a neurotic, she is psychopathic — she badly needs expert treatment. I realize you feel sensitive about it but you don't want her condition to deteriorate. Matters could become dangerous."

"Come on now, David, she's neurotic, I grant you . . ." Peter bit at the inside of his lip, "but you can't make me believe she'd ever be harmful." He gave a dry laugh, "it's too absurd. Beautiful, gentle Ann."

"Your 'beautiful, gentle Ann' can ruin your sons' lives and make no mistake about it."

"Christ! Now *you* sound as if you need psychiatric treatment."

David decided it was his duty to speak out. "Peter — I'm sorry to tell you that in my opinion, Ann is wildly in love with both Roy and Nicky."

Peter's dark eyebrows drew into a straight line above his brown eyes burning with disgust. "What an unmitigatedly revolting assumption! You dare accuse Ann of being incestuous!"

"Your surprised reaction astonishes me. My God, man, surely you've suspected this. It's fundamental medical knowledge that a child is entirely primitive until taught to lay aside childish ways and to sublimate unacceptable behaviour until he turns into someone people will live with. Quite often the process fails and neurosis develops. I think Ann is a case of this. A parent is the first person a child relates to and this can set the pattern for all other relationships. My guess is she was mad about her tall blond father and she's transferred this love to your sons

64

— there are people who are obsessed by 'family looks'. She was mad about her father wasn't she?"

Peter was mentally steeling himself to face facts. "Yes, he was an exceptionally handsome man — my boys resemble him, but for God's sake, David, that doesn't mean that . . ."

"It adds up, Peter. She was mad about her father, and when her mother died she was his constant companion and acted as his hostess when he was Ambassador in France. She never even contemplated marriage until after his death — only then did she accept you. It fits the pattern."

Peter angrily shook his head. "It's bloody rot! I'm telling you, all bloody rot." But too well he recalled his wedding night when Ann had not permitted him to touch her. It was only after two weeks of their honeymoon in Venice that she had allowed him to consummate the marriage. Christ! had she been comparing him, dark and five-foot-eight, with her blond elegantly tall father? He shook his head as if to rid it of a constricting band. "It's got to be rot, David, we've been happily married for years."

"Have you?" David asked quietly. "On the level? Listen we're such old friends that I'll confide in you. My wife — Margaret — is utterly frigid. The whole performance is a boresome duty to her. Her attitude came as a bloody shock to me because before marriage she enjoyed petting, and I believed she refused to go all the way because of moral reasons. What a laugh! She had been seduced in her teens and hated it but she wanted to be married and found me suitable to be her husband — on her terms. They were, 'once-a-week-to-oblige-you-David'. Well, that routine soon bored hell out of me. I need a responsive bed companion. So for years I've taken my pleasure elsewhere."

David's confession loosened a little of Peter's deeply buried thoughts about Ann. "It's not like that with us. I've always been madly in love with Ann and, whilst I regretted that she's not a sexual woman — I've never strayed because the truth is I'm still mad about her."

Poor sod, David thought, knowing too well how a certain type of woman could ruin even a strong man. "Tell me when did these 'illnesses' of hers start?"

Peter threw his mind back trying to pinpoint the first time. "About five years ago I guess, at Sports Day at the boys' school. Between them Roy and Nicky had gathered up most of the sports awards as well as some academic prizes. Ann and I were like pouter pigeons with pride, then as we were about to leave for New York the boys introduced us to a couple of 'teenage sisters. Pretty kids, they were staying the night in the nearby town to go dancing with the boys — well, without warning Ann collapsed in a faint against Nicky. Luckily he caught her before she hit the floor."

"Ah ha," David nodded and sipped his drink, "what then?"

"I concluded it was the excitement that had been too much for her, anyhow she opened those God-damn fantastic eyes of hers and whispered, 'I want the boys to return to New York with me'. Naturally they did and going back she recovered almost completely."

The evil bitch, David thought. "Roy and Nicky were then about seventeen and eighteen?" he said.

"Yeah, and marvellous looking guys, it was then that Ann started to call them 'My wonderful golden sons'!"

"Didn't it strike you that her affection was a bit . . . well . . . a bit excessive?"

"Of course not! It was a natural motherly pride, it isn't as if she wanted to maul them, only wanted them with her."

Peter must be losing his grip, David thought. "I'm afraid I'm not so nice-minded,

I would have read more into it than that," he said. "She put up this mock faint to cut the boys' dates with the pretty sisters. Doesn't that make you suspicious?"

"Oh Christ, David!" Peter said indignantly, "you've been in Hollywood too much, and the crooked thinking has got you. Most normal mothers go a bit overboard for their sons when they start growing into manhood."

"Peter, I have plenty of *normal* mother patients," David smiled, "even in Hollywood and Beverly Hills, so I know about them. But, at dinner at your place I witnessed something absolutely horrible when Ann lay into that little Karyn girl whom Roy is obviously wild about. When Ann had almost demolished Karyn she pulled a typical psycho trick by collapsing. If you'll only listen to my advice you'll get Ann the best treatment in the country — she needs it."

Van Buren felt deeply despondent. "Do you advise me to put off our European trip? That would upset Ann more than you can imagine."

"It's for two months . . . and she'll have her sons with her so perhaps things will be okay for that duration but, don't fool yourself, Peter, when you return you've got to get her into the care of a psychiatrist. Roy and Nicky have reached marriageable age and she's growing desperate in case she loses them; besides her condition can lead to duodenal ulcer, hypertension and other illnesses but, Christ, you're a doctor, I don't have to tell *you* all this!"

Van Buren sighed deeply, then banged his empty glass down on a nearby table. "It smells of failure — failure — failure! It stinks!" He was quiet whilst a nearby wall clock chimed five times. "I must go, David — must look in at my Clinic. I amputated a ten year old boy's leg yesterday. Cancer — bloody awful business."

"Yeah, man — that's *real* trouble!"

"Right. Well I'm glad we've had this chat, we'll meet again I hope before we fly off and I'll arrange for Ann to start treatments as soon as we return from Europe."

They shook hands and parted then David dismissed Van Buren from his mind and went to make a telephone call.

Enjoying the sight of the luxurious shop windows, Joan strolled happily along Fifth Avenue, her lunch with her agent at glamorous "Caravelle" had been a success, for he had told her a publisher had accepted her last novel and the payment when signing the contract would be generous. What a relief, for now she could shoulder more of the monthly expenses. Money was not coming in easily for poor Moira.

It was past four when she returned to the apartment, went to her room and gladly slipped her shoes off, then stretched out on the bed. Lord, how lucky she was to have her talent to write, she pitied widows obliged to fill their lives with card games. She was lucky, too, that Moira and Karyn needed her, yet she had lonely moments when she missed a close male companion.

Then her eyes fell closed whilst far below the drone of traffic added to the wine she had drunk at lunch, sent her off into contented sleep. The brash telephone bell awakened her. Still half asleep she reached beside her for the receiver, then settled against the pillows and said, "Hello."

A man's voice. "Is Mrs Clements there?"

She hesitated a moment, the voice dug sharply down into her cave of memories. "Who wants her please?"

A hesitation, she could feel the caller's tension coming through the 'phone. "Well, I'm an old friend . . ."

Good God! she *knew* that rough, rather hoarse voice! "Yes, yes," she murmured as she shivered, whilst waiting to be assured that memory was not lying.

"My name is . . . but — say . . . Joan, is that *you?*"

"Yes, yes . . . David . . . it is."

"Good God!"

"Yes . . . you're right — good God!"

Eight

Joan stared at her reflection in the dressing table mirror. What would David see when he arrived? A still attractive middle-aged woman with wide staring eyes. *Why*, in God's name, *why* had she accepted his dinner invitation? She was mad! But how could she have helped it? She wanted desperately to see him once more.

Anyhow *he* would not look like the man she had been insanely in love with — he also would be marked by the years. What luck that she had just had her hair done for the lunch with her agent. It was still thick — still a rich gold. Thank God her eyes and skin were still good. She yanked a dress of a pinky-beige from its hanger and stepped into it. Pinky-beige had been his favourite colour for her.

She hurried to the kitchen to get ice out, filled the icebucket then took it to the living-room. She turned only a couple of lamps on. He must see her again in the kindest light that would soften the spite of time. There was the buzzer! He was at the hall door! She forced herself to walk slowly to admit him. Her trembling hands fumbled the locks, then she gulped in some air and pulled the door open to look up at a tall, well built man, his dark hair going prey. He smiled a bit diffidently as the blue-blue eyes — yes, they *were* the same — searched her face.

For a moment they stared at each other across twenty-five years of tears, laughter, loving, which so foolishly they had not shared. Despite her age he found her still beautiful and he thanked God for it.

"Joan — it's good to see you again."

"Oh David — it's good to see *you* again."

Another pause, a time for their eyes to absorb each other, then he said, "May I come in or are you condemning me to the mat for misbehaviour?"

Then they laughed together; that was something they had shared so much of — laughter. "Come in, come in, you've not misbehaved as far as I know."

As he followed her into the living-room, his eyes swept over her figure, still slim and graceful. "I've brought you something you used to like." He handed her a package.

"How kind of you, David — please sit down." He sat next to her on the sofa watching her undo the gold ribbon, then take the gold paper off. Swathed in protective cotton wool were two bottles of champagne, "*Pink Champagne!* Oh, no!" It was like her dream. "I can't believe it! How wonderful that you remembered."

"Oh, I recall untold things that happened between us." His voice was so deliberately meaningful that the blood flew to her face. Absurd! Impossible that he was remembering their lovemaking. To hide her nervousness she burst out, "How clever of you — you bought chilled champagne so we can drink some at once." She sprang up handing him a bottle, "Do open it, I'll get the glasses."

Watching his long sun-tanned fingers expertly uncork the bottle, she held the glasses out to him and he carefully poured the rosy dancing liquid into them. Then they clinked glasses.

"To us," he said, a puzzled look in his eyes.

They sipped the champagne and Joan sat down, "I can't quite believe this is happening — it's too odd, you see, some days ago, I dreamed we were lunching together and drinking pink champagne —"

"Strange — because last week I came across a novel of yours in a Beverly Hills store and wondered, as I have done for years — where you were."

"I think it's a perfect demonstration of telepathy, but how did you get my 'phone number?"

"From your grand-daughter, at the Van Buren dinner party."

"Oh! The little minx didn't tell me she'd met you, but she left the next day for the mountains whilst I was still asleep. You know, David, you've changed very little."

She was being utterly sincere. Of course the lean face was lined but that added character to it, the wide humorous mouth with strong slightly uneven teeth — she might have seen it yesterday, and above all — those blue blue eyes!

"You haven't changed much either, Joan." He stood looking down at her. "You must have discovered the fountain of youth."

"Mad flattery — I look like the *mother* of that girl you were in . . ." She broke off just in time to swallow the word 'love', but he went on.

"The girl I was in love with — you were going to say?" He sipped his champagne, surprised at himself for being so stirred by her, for he had not come here for any emotional involvement but merely to renew an old friendship. Yet her warm personality, her marvellously expressive eyes, her soft English voice were definitely reaching out to him again. But no danger in that — he and she were now sensible middle-aged people. "You know, I think part of our trouble was that we were too much in love," he said.

"God knows how I dug up the courage to leave for London but I felt I had to cut everything between us or we'd destroy each other." She sipped her champagne, there was a macabre pleasure in reliving the sadness — not alone — but with him.

"I guess you were years ahead of Women's Lib." There was a shadow of tenderness in his smile. "Despite your gentleness you were the most dominating little bitch God ever created. I think I resented being in love so much and I rebelled against your hold on me. Look at it from my viewpoint, I was two years out of Harvard Medical — it had been a helluva sacrifice for my corn-belt parents to foot that expense — then I had the luck to land a place in a top Hollywood Clinic with the whole world — or so I stupidly thought — spread out before me and I was hell bent to be a big success! To have my own Clinic someday. All this meant that there was no place in my set-up to be in love with a beautiful young divorcee whose ex was one of the top men in films and could put a spoke in my wheel if he'd a mind to."

"And added to it all you were chased by

most of the Hollywood stars ready to lay their fortunes and themselves at your feet," Joan said. She was surprised at how the memories still had power to hurt her. "Of course over the years I've come to understand that," she went on, "and I've often regretted that I had absolutely no sympathy with your problems, I've often wanted to say, 'David, I'm sorry I was so unkind', — well at last — I've said it." As he sat beside her on the couch she stared into his eyes going almost black with tenseness.

"Thanks . . . it's good to know that at last you understand."

"I'm glad," she whispered, strangely relieved in her heart. "I'm also glad that you got your clinic."

"Ah, and through my *own* efforts, I didn't need a woman's money, although my wife happens to be wealthy."

"Yes, Hollywood friends wrote to me in London saying you'd married a San Francisco girl — with a fortune."

"That was several years after I heard about your marriage in London."

She stretched her green eyes wide with teasing surprise. "It was chivalrous of you to wait, David." Funny how his marriage still had power to hurt her. "But to be serious, I should congratulate you, you are such a famous doctor now. That must be a very satisfying feeling."

"Sure is, and you're due for congratulations too, you've done well with your writing." From an inner pocket of his grey mohair jacket he brought out a slim gold cigarette case. As he opened it she stared at it in amazement. God! It could not be true! It was the case she had given him a quarter of a century ago. He held it open to her, his eyes fixed on hers.

"Is it . . . the . . . the one . . . ?"

He nodded. "The same. I've always been most attached to it."

"But the old inscription?"

"Look for yourself."

She glanced inside the gold cover and read, in a facsimile of her writing, 'From J — Toujours Means Always'.

Tears sprang to her eyes but angry with her weakness she blinked them away. "But your — your wife?"

He gave a little shrug of indifference. "Margaret doesn't mind; she's never jealous, that's one of the reasons why I married her, a quiet, calm woman — quite emotionless, ideal for a woman specialist's wife. She never even wanted children to disturb her own routine — so we've had no heights — no depths. You know, after you went out of my life, all my thoughts went to medicine."

"Rather like me since I've been widowed, my writing has become almost my whole life." She spoke thoughtfully, "I suppose it all adds up to the sad truth that love is a form of madness — that so often weakens people."

"By God! I never thought I'd hear *you,* the great 'romantic' talk like that. You, who always maintained that love was the greatest human force — money, fame, position were nothing — love was *all!*"

A corkscrew type of a laugh came up her throat. "Yes, and so it used to be with me, remember the way I trekked every weekend during the war to that awful one-horse town, San Luis Obispo, when you were stationed at the army hospital at that huge camp."

"Yes, by God, you were wonderful."

"And those two shabby hotels, always full, so I found that funny little apartment, do you remember when the furniture didn't arrive on time, that first weekend we had to sleep on a mattress on the floor." She started to laugh and he joined in.

"Right, and we had supper of sardines out of a can, but don't forget how I found a store that sold pink champagne."

"Oh nothing ever tasted more delicious

than those sardines and pink champagne out of paper cups." They laughed with a joyous type of abandon of young people as they relived the magic of those nights.

Then Joan stood up — she could bear no more — remembrances were choking her with a longing to relive the past. She moved to a window to look out at the glittering sight of giant buildings with windows aglow. She breathed deeply, trying to regain her calm.

He stood looking at her back, straight, slim as a young woman's. He could recall what she looked like naked. By God! Impossible that some kind of love for her was still buried so deeply in him.

She turned and stood staring up at him with sadness in her big eyes, and suddenly his arms went around her and he kissed her uplifted mouth. She returned the pressure of his lips, her heart thumping against his chest. Immediately his arms crushed her to his hard body. Now he kissed her with some of his long ago passion.

For marvellous minutes they stood in each other's arms, bodies closely touching, lips clinging to each other's. Then she broke away.

"Open the other bottle of champagne, David! Let's *really* celebrate — forget about dinner," she laughed. "We can eat dinner any time — but this special night will never come again."

"By God! It's *you!* I've really found you again!"

Nine

One morning, down at Carl's small boat-house at the lake surrounded by mountains in the Adirondacks, Karyn and Roy dragged out his putt-putt boat, settled the fishing gear and lunch into it, then launched it on to the lake's placid water.

As they moved toward the centre of the lake Karyn said, "We really are the only two living creatures in this world up here. In the past three days that we've been here we've not seen another living being."

"You mean a *human* being, but we've seen plenty of deer, squirrels, hares, rabbits — beetles . . ."

"Of course, silly, I meant people."

"But, I go for the loneliness — I haven't missed seeing people, have you?"

"Terribly," she laughed. "Haven't you noticed?" She leaned over the side of the boat, trailing her hand in the water. "It will soon be warm enough for swimming."

"Work first — fun later. We gotta get some fish — so at least I feel I've done *something*. Do you realise I've not cracked a book up here — all we've done is . . ."

"Make super-super-super love under the kind eyes of Whiteface Mountain, Pulpit Mountain and McKenzie." She waved around at the mountain peaks.

"Say Nugget, I've got a good idea —" said Roy suddenly, "I'll 'phone you everyday when I'm in Europe."

Karyn felt sick at the reminder that they were to be parted but she said, "To hear your voice will be a help."

"Yeah, for me too. We'll make a date — I'll call you at cocktail time which will be two o'clock New York time — okay? Good — now, how about taking the trout rods out?"

She started to untie the strings on the green canvas bags then carefully pulled the slim rods out and handed them to him. She sat staring across the flat water to the dark, heavily wooded hills and mountain peaks. "Let's come back here for our *real* honeymoon, shall we?"

"You bet, Mrs Van Buren."

"Oh, that sounds so wonderful! I'd like to be called Mrs *Viking* Van Buren — is it somehow possible?"

"Sure, why not?" He grinned at her anxious expression, "I'll record my name as Viking and marry you as Viking Van Buren."

"That's great! It's such a wonderful name,

isn't it? Listen! I'll shout it out aloud." She cupped her mouth with her hands, took a deep breath then, in measured tones like an ancient herald she intoned.

"VI . . . KING . . . VAN . . . BU . . . REN!"

Within seconds the distant echo floated back to them as they looked solemnly at each other, and she cupped her mouth to call again but he said, "Quit it Nugget, it's kinda creepy. Makes me feel I'm being summoned to some eerie gathering."

"No, no, darling. I was establishing your name for all time."

"Okay, okay, but I bet you sure as hell have frightened the trout off. You've a curious mystic side to you, haven't you?"

"I suppose I get it from Grans — she was born in Limerick, where everyone believed in leprechauns."

"You're a bit of a leprechaun yourself." He laughed, loving the look of her, particularly when her green eyes seemed filled with mystery. "Now honey, be absolutely silent so the fish will bite."

"I'll put the Irish camithera on the trout," she whispered.

But, after hours of waiting for a nibble, Roy said, "I guess the fish didn't get your signal so let's call it a day."

"Okay, slave driver, the sun's going down, it's not warm enough for a swim now."

At the cottage when they were in the living-room drinking beer Karyn's eyes rested on him and she told herself, there could never be another guy who looked like him — he had it all. This golden, out-door, athletic look, mixed with the gentle, kind look of a priest — as she had so often seen it on his face.

"Oh Viking — I wish nothing would ever change. I'd love us to be always as we are now — I wish we could stay here like this for ever." She suddenly sank on her knees and laid her head on his lap.

He ran his fingers through her thick hair. "I read a poem once, about this man who was so in love that he made a bargain with Fate that he would give his life from the age of forty-five on if the girl could always keep the beauty and youth of her twenty-first year. I thought it was crap then — now I guess I almost understand it. But, up with you — I must do some of that medical reading."

"Okay, and I'll get dinner."

After cornbeef hash and hash-brown potatoes, salad, cherry pie and ice cream, Roy settled down to study and Karyn sat on the floor, back against the wall, reading Dame Margot Fonteyn's book on ballet.

It was ten o'clock when Roy snapped his volume shut, then yawned and stretched. "Hey, Nugget, how about some shut-eye?"

"Okay — I'll just shower — or do you want to first?"

Later they climbed into bed and Roy gathered her into his arms. Then after making passionate love he resolved that from now on he would make it his job to see that she was always cared for and happy.

Ten

Their wonderful week was over and, though feeling utterly miserable, Karyn tried to be jocular. "Windows locked, electricity turned off at the main, house spick and span by courtesy of Viking and his devoted Nugget." Inside herself she was weeping. "It's awful having to go back — I feel like we're leaving our first home together."

She climbed into the Porsche and Roy drove off, hating to go and eager to be quit of this crazy feeling of bereavement.

The cottage was already behind them when he said, "Don't feel low, Nugget, the great time we've had up there is a sample of what our life together is going to be like."

"Oh, Viking, I can't help feeling low. I hate this old European trip of yours, but I'm going to work madly whilst you're away," she laughed with a tremor in her throat, "and entrepreneurs will say, 'this girl is star material, she'll be a great ballerina!' When you return you'll come to see me dance a *pas de deux* with — with — Baryshnikov!" She ended on a sigh — "oh Viking I can't think about anything else but that at noon tomorrow — *you* leave — I can't bear to talk about it any more." She rested her head on his shoulder.

Later when Karyn was home she left her suitcase in the hall and found her grandmother in the drawing-room sitting with Doctor Murdoch.

"Well! Doc Murdoch! What a nice surprise!" Karyn turned with a guilty face to Joan, "So sorry, Grans, I never told you I'd met up with Doc."

"That's okay Karyn," David said. "You see I've found my way here. And how did you like the Adirondacks?"

"Oh, it was beautiful up there — New York's so shabby to come back to."

"It's not my favourite place once summer comes," Joan said, then smiled widely. "Look, darling, how spoiled I am. Doctor Murdoch brings me pink champagne every night — do have some."

"I'd love some Grans." She felt near to tears about Roy's imminent departure. She and he had agreed not to say goodbye in person, but over the 'phone where she could cry in private. She took the glass of champagne which David handed her and felt she must say something. "I'm so glad you're still in New York. When do you go back to California?"

"In a couple of days, I've several medical meetings lined up here first. Where are you two going this summer?" he asked Joan.

"We've made no plans yet. Moira usually takes short, sporadic holidays, but Karyn and I have gone several times to Cape Cod and Martha's Vineyard."

"Then make a change and come out to my ranch. It's in northern California — a most beautiful spot. I've got some decent horses so you can ride and swimming is good." He was staring down intently at Joan. It was to be an experiment which he had already decided to make, to give himself time with her, to test if this resuscitated love he felt for her was stable, not just lightly emotional. "Count on staying at least three weeks."

It sounded God-sent to Joan and her big eyes were round with surprise. "But, Margaret — I mean your wife doesn't even know us."

"Oh, forget about her — she hates even the idea of the ranch, never been to see it, she prefers the sea. She and her brother sail together all summer — messing around Mexican waters. I'm mainly alone on the ranch, so it would be great if you two came." His blue eyes went dark with appeal to Joan.

"Well . . . it sounds wonderful." The bliss

of three weeks with David and out of New York's heat. "Karyn, darling, would you like to go?"

"Yes thanks, Gran — but, Doc, have you a 'phone on the ranch? I've *gotta* be near a 'phone."

Joan and David both looked at her in surprise and he said, "Naturally I have a 'phone, but you sound like a doctor. Why ever do you need to be near a 'phone?"

"Someone will be 'phoning me every day and I'd die sooner than miss the call."

"Well then, as you'll have a 'phone I take it that you both accept. When will you come? The sooner, the better."

Joan's eyes felt misty, he really seemed to want them. "Shall we say the end of July?"

"That's great!" David's relieved grin still had power after twenty-five years to make Joan's heart quicken.

"Oh, I'll just get my address book, I'll need the 'phone number on the ranch." Karyn left the room.

Joan and David exchanged surprised glances and Joan asked, "Whyever does she need the number now?"

"Young Van Buren. He's off to Europe tomorrow."

"Ah yes, that's why she seems low, poor pet."

When Karyn had written the number in her book she said, "Excuse me please — I've got a headache."

"Of course, darling," Joan said, then glanced at David. "Would you mind if we don't go out to dinner. I'll whip up something here; I don't like leaving Karyn when she's just come home."

"No — no, Grans, please go . . ."

"Of course we won't leave Karyn," David said, smiling into her eyes, "as a Doctor, I say the very best thing for Karyn's headache is to come out with us to Quo Vadis — I'll 'phone them and instruct them to change our table from two to three."

The next morning Roy telephoned Karyn from the airport to say goodbye and somehow she managed not to weep. She told him she would be going to David's ranch and gave him the telephone number. Then finding the agony almost unbearable, she gasped, "I love you — I love you Viking, but I'm going to hang up," and she did, then she dashed to her room to lie on her bed weeping into her pillow.

The next day it was arranged between Joan and Moira that Joan would pay the expensive fees for Karyn's ballet lessons and Karyn started training. Work, work, work, was the only thing to help her during Roy's absence.

Roy's daily telephone calls from the capitals of Europe were her life line. She existed to hear his voice assuring her of his love and how he was missing her. She refused all dates excepting an occasional evening out with Carl when he left Boston for New York. He was missing Claudine and it relieved him to be able to rant to Karyn against Mrs Van Buren for having whisked Claudine away.

So time dragged by with Karyn ticking off the days on a calendar in her room.

Joan and Moira were growing anxious about her and Moira confidentially told her mother, "She's really suffering over Roy's absence — it worries me. Too bad he's not marriage-minded. Oh Lord, what a break it would be for her, if only he were."

"Well, he's still pretty young and David was saying that Mrs Van Buren is a very possessive mother and a difficult woman," Joan said. "He believes Roy and Karyn are in love and I think he was tactfully trying to warn me that they would run into difficulties with his mother."

"Who cares about her!" Moira snapped, "If Roy *wants* to marry Karyn he'll do it. According to what one reads, all the Van Buren clan have been left fortunes in Trust. Roy could easily borrow against his inheritance and marry when he likes." She sighed,

"I guess he's just not keen enough."

"Well, we don't know about that, but he 'phones her everyday, religiously, to tell her how he loves her and misses her. She seems to exist for the calls, poor little thing."

"Hm . . . m, letters would be better, writing lives. Oh well, my nice, high-powered lawyer, Len Rockwell, flew in from Texas, so I'll be late again tonight. We're going to a big Republican dinner; he's mad on politics. Come and sit with me whilst I dress."

In Moira's bedroom, Joan settled into an armchair as Moira pulled off her dress. "Is Rocky thinking of running for Congress?" Joan asked.

"No — I think he's interested in the Senate. He's made a considerable fortune at Corporation Law so, of course, he could afford to take time off to serve his country; he hasn't said so, it's just something I assume. Anyhow, I love being with him, he's such a welcome change from the Broadway show people." Moira sat at the dressing-table, brushing her short, dark, curly hair.

"I can well understand that, and he certainly seems keen on you, judging by all the flowers he sends and the way he's always taking you out."

"Yes, I think he's keen on me," Moira said a little longingly, visualising the tall

93

Texan with deep-set hazel eyes and rock-like features, so reminiscent of Abraham Lincoln. "But there are stumbling blocks — Rocky is married — remember?"

"I do." Joan nodded sympathetically. "Does the marriage work?"

"I don't know. I try to steer clear of the subject and Rocky seldom mentions his wife, just says she had a bad time when their son was killed in Vietnam — their only child."

"Terrible for Rocky, as well as her."

"Yeah." Moira started to cream her face. "But, what's new with Doc Murdoch?"

"Oh, he's back in New York for the week-end."

"It's one for the books, the way you and he have picked up where you left off years ago."

"What nonsense, we're only old friends."

"Oh Mother, tell that to the marines." Moira laughed into the looking-glass at Joan. "He flies into town every week-end to see you. That spells more than friendship to me. I remember when I was a kid how mad you were about each other. I liked him — he was fun."

"He's explained to me how his marriage works. He and his wife lead separate personal lives but stay publicly married because she likes having an escort for social events, also she likes maintaining a large establishment. I've known lots of women like that. Anyhow, don't you start getting ideas about an Indian Summer romance for me." Joan stood up, she was too embarrassed to let Moira guess what a rebirth it was for her to have David back in her life with the diffident, half puzzled look in his eyes when he said, 'By God, Joan, I think I'm falling in love with you again'.

She shook Moira's dress out and, as she went to hang it in the closet, she said, "Anyhow, I'm delighted he invited us to his ranch. It will be good for Karyn to be out of New York and in the country. I only wish you could come with us. You need a holiday badly."

"Don't worry, I'll be okay — I'll be going down to Cape Cod. I've some artists in the little theatre down there."

"Good. Well, thank heavens it's only three more days until we leave New York. I can't wait to escape the heat."

Eleven

David closed the car door as Joan settled into the passenger seat, with Karyn in the back. He got into the driver's seat and started the white Mercedes, edging it out of the parking area of San Francisco airport.

"It's great that you two beautiful girls are here." David gave a satisfied little chuckle, "I had a hunch that you might change your minds at the last moment and not come."

"Oh no!" Joan burst out, "we've been longing to come."

"We sure have Doc, New York is like a furnace." Karyn liked him even more in his pale blue and navy sports clothes. "We couldn't wait to get away," she giggled, "and to see you."

"Well, that's nice to hear, the temperature's fine here, but just wait until we get into the country."

It was when they had left the City's outskirts and were travelling down a country road that Karyn moved forward to lean on the back of the front seat.

"This is lovely Doc, the far off mountain peaks remind me of Switzerland."

"Yes, parts of it are like Switzerland, but our trees surpass anything that grows there."

For another half an hour they drove through the beautiful wooded countryside, then the Mercedes slowly climbed up a rough narrow road where a wrought-iron sign read, 'Aurora Ranch'. Around a couple of turns and David's house came into view. Mexican style, it was a spreading bungalow type, with cream adobe walls topped by a brilliant red-tiled roof. David pulled up before the six tiled steps leading to the wide porch and they all got out.

"Oh, how lovely it is! How serenely peaceful." The words came tumbling from Joan's happy heart as she stared out across a wide vista of undulating green land, dotted with clumps of huge trees.

"Yeah — I was lucky, the ranch was a gift to me from a grateful patient of many years. An old widow, Mrs Doherty, she was crazy about the place and bequeathed it to me. That was six years ago."

"Wowie, Doc — what a gift!" Karyn exclaimed.

"I'll say. It's become such a wonderful refuge for me that I'll never part with it."

What a spoilt bitch his wife must be, Joan thought, never to have bothered to even visit the place. "Who named it 'Aurora Ranch', David, did you?"

"No, Mrs Doherty's grandfather, more than a hundred years ago. It's well named — Aurora means dawn and the moment night disappears the rising sun strikes the house. I also inherited a splendid couple in Mr and Mrs Ryan as housekeeper, caretaker. It was a condition of Mrs Doherty's will that I keep them on. Now let's go in and relax."

The large shadowy living-room was built in Mexican style — white stucco walls, at one end a huge fireplace with heavy wrought-iron fittings, furniture of dark wood studded with silver-headed nails. Brilliantly coloured Mexican rugs partly covered the red tile floor.

"What a good aura this room has," Joan said, as she sank into a wide chair with worn leather seat.

"I've left everything the way I found it," said David, "except for books. I brought some favourites up here." He went to a dark heavily carved cabinet, "Okay, orders for drinks."

"Scotch please," said Joan.

"Coke, for me please," said Karyn, "but Doc, where's the 'phone, I don't see it in here?"

"Don't worry, it's in the hall," David

laughed. "You won't miss Roy's call."

"How come you know that *he's* going to call?"

"Honey, do you think I'm blind? At the Van Burens' you and Roy had eyes for no one but each other. Nothing wrong with being in love. I'm a great rooter for Romance, despite my grey hairs." He shot a grin at Joan. "Believe it or not, *I've* been in love, I know what it's like." He gave Joan her scotch, then a coke to Karyn. "Welcome to Aurora Ranch." He raised his glass to Joan and his blue eyes were dark with intensity; he could hardly make himself believe she was actually sitting in the room, looking so lovely.

Momentarily she lost herself in the warmth of his eyes. "Thank you for inviting us, David."

"I've planned some side trips which I hope you'll like. We'll start off early in the morning, then . . ."

"But, Doc," Karyn interrupted, "the thing is I'm not sure what time Roy's calls will come through — you know Europe is eight hours ahead of California so if he continues to call me at six European time it will be ten A.M. here." Her big eyes and her entire being appealed to David for understanding. "Please forgive me — but I've just gotta be

99

here, which might mess up your plans."

"Don't look so worried," David smiled reassuringly. "When he calls tomorrow tell him to switch his time in future so that he comes through seven or eight A.M. our time."

"But he mightn't be able to — he calls at cocktail time so he won't upset his mother's timetable."

"God dammit, Karyn, the best thing for Roy to do is to tell his mother he's in love with you. Make her face up to that and the crazy woman will be a helluva lot better off."

Karyn was at first astonished, then gratified to know that an eminent Doctor shared her feelings about Mrs Van Buren. "Yes, I think you're right, but just the same I must be here for his call tomorrow." She threw an appealing glance at Joan, "Is that okay?"

"Oh, I think it will be," Joan said gently as her big eyes swung toward David's amused-looking face. "Have you made plans for anything before ten tomorrow?"

"I was going to take you riding for a couple of hours over my land, then be back for lunch."

"But why don't you and Grans go without me?"

"David," Joan laughed, "I've not ridden for years. You're an optimist to think I could ride for a couple of hours."

"But, sometimes you enjoyed being in the saddle for hours, riding around San Luis Obispo."

She nodded, "That's true, but I was much younger then. Well we'll see, maybe I'll do better on a horse than I think."

"Why, did you two ride in San Luis Obispo, Grans? I thought it's supposed to be dull scenery."

"You're right, it's certainly *not* a beauty spot," Joan told Karyn. "David was stationed at the hospital in the huge Army Camp at San Luis Obispo during the war and I sometimes visited him."

"Oh yeah," Karyn nodded understandingly. "It must have been tough for you, Grans — thinking that at any moment he might be shipped out to the war zone."

"David, may I go to my room? I feel rather bedraggled," asked Joan to end the conversation.

"You bet, I'll just bring your baggage from the car."

"I'll help you Doc," and Karyn went with him. As he opened the boot of the Mercedes she stood beside him, and murmured a little fearfully, "Doc, I guess I should tell you that Grans told me that you two were in love once, and I think it's swell that you've met up again."

Surprised, a little annoyed, he could not find any suitable words and muttered, "Well, thanks, Karyn."

"You know she works too hard and she needs to rest. Why don't you make her stay awhile — I mean after I've gone . . . but why do you look at me like that, Doc? Are you angry I asked about Grans staying on?"

"Hell, no! I'd love her to stay on for as long as she likes but, I promise you she won't stay without you."

"That's a laugh! Am I playing chaperone to Grans?"

"I guess you are. I'm old enough to be your father — even your grandfather, so *she's* not chaperoning *you*."

"I wish you *were* my grandfather, I never knew him, he died before I came along." Karyn suddenly felt quite tearful. "I wish you were my Grandfather and I wish that you and Grans . . ." she broke off.

"Whatever happened to you two?" Joan asked as she came out onto the porch and David and Karyn hurried up with the bags. Then the telephone rang.

"Oh damn! I'll bet that's my Clinic and I told them not to call except for an emergency." David strode into the hall and grabbed the receiver, "Aurora Ranch." A pause. "Yes — hold on, she's right here. Karyn!"

She flew into the hall and grabbed the receiver. "Viking!"

"Nugget — hiya. Trip okay from New York? Just wanted to check on my girl."

"Oh, that's *wonderful* — just *wonderful!* I never expected you to call me here today."

"We're in London now, at Claridges, and we're played out, with all this moving around, and Claudine is stoned most of the time. Thank God Carl flies in tomorrow, he'll help get her off the pot. How's it there, sugar?"

"Just beautiful — all green and quiet; you'll love it. Oh Viking, I'm counting every day until you're back and, oh! could you call me at eight A.M. our time in future. Doc has planned to take us out on day trips."

"You bet, honey — you know the time here?"

"No, darling."

"Three A.M. but I couldn't sleep, I had to make sure you were okay."

"Thank you, darling. Go to sleep now, I'm *always, always* thinking of you, 'Nite, darling, God bless you."

"I love you, Nugget — 'nite."

Across six thousand miles the beloved voice comforted her. Then she heard the

103

click that separated them, and the distance dividing them hammered her consciousness like a blow. So far — away — he . . .

Suddenly there was a tightness around her throat and she felt sick. Excitement, she guessed, and went back to the living-room where Joan and David smiled benignly at her.

"That was Roy — he's in London." She sank into a chair, "I don't know what it is, but I feel awful — I guess it's something I've eaten — the crevette on the plane — maybe . . ."

Suddenly the room, her grandmother's face and the Doctor's swirled about her and blackness submerged her.

David scooped her up in his arms. "I'll put her on to her bed."

Terribly anxious, Joan followed them. "She's never fainted before! Maybe it's food poisoning, and she's been dancing for hours every day in the heat. She's overdone it."

"She's an emotional kid — isn't she?"

"Very sensitive," Joan said tremulously, terribly upset at seeing Karyn unconscious.

David put Karyn on the bed, saying, "Loosen her bra and belt, I'll get some spirits of ammonia."

Within seconds of inhaling the spirits of ammonia, Karyn's eyelids fluttered open.

Staring perplexedly up at Joan, then at David looking down at her, she murmured, "What gives?"

"You passed out, honey. How are you feeling now?" David's fingers were checking her pulse.

"A bit sick."

"It's all the excitement of catching the 'plane on time." Joan gently smoothed her forehead, "and then Roy's 'phone call."

"I guess that's it, Grans."

"Well, she seems healthy enough." David looked reassuringly across the bed at Joan, then he grinned teasingly, "What a surprise for Roy when he knows his call made you pass out — eh Karyn? That's love, I guess."

Joan and Karyn were glad to be able to smile.

Twelve

After Joan and Karyn had been ten days on the ranch, David knew that his experiment of being constantly with Joan now proved beyond doubt that he was again in love with her. It was unbelievable, incredible how deeply and tenderly he felt about her. For the first time in many years he knew happiness.

Now as they strolled on the edge of the woods, waiting for Karyn and Ryan, the-man-of-all work who ran the ranch, to gallop past them, David told Joan exactly how he felt about her.

She was deeply stirred, ready to shout with happiness, then cry with sorrow, for he had a wife who separated them. "David, you must know of course that I feel about you as I always have. It's impossible to credit that meeting you again should blot out all the years we were apart. Do you think it's because our affair was never *ended?* I mean — it was broken off at its height and put into deep freeze." She gave a tremulous laugh, "You could say that meeting again has defrosted everything."

"Yeah, I have no explanation for the whole strange business excepting, I suppose, if you've always loved strawberries and cream — it doesn't mean because you've been denied them for a period that you won't be mad about them when you're offered them again."

She laughed happily. "A wonderful way of describing the strange business."

"But what about Basil? You must have loved him; I know you so well, you would never have married him otherwise."

"You're right — I did love him — but quite differently. My love for you was so strong, so exhausting, but nothing killed it. Even though I believed we should never meet again, I put my love for you in cotton wool as something infinitely precious to be preserved. But I had a very happy life with Basil. He approved of me in every way — which was very satisfactory."

"That's the difference between us, I never had a happy life with Margaret. Oh, she manages a house excellently, entertains splendidly for me and at first we shared quite a few interests and had many mutual friends. But there was never any love between us; it was more like a good friendship. Then she became interested in charity work and devoted more and more of her time to that, which separated us even further, then when she was asked on to the Committee for Vietnam Refugees she lost herself in that heart and soul. We share the same house but don't often meet each other."

"A sad, loveless existence, it seems to me, but what about your private life? I don't mean to be presumptuous, but I can't see you living like a monk."

"You're right, honey, it's not my line," he chuckled, "Margaret's attitude freed me to do as I pleased, I think you really spoiled me for all women — your warmth, your affection — no one was capable of loving me as you did. Now, thank God, I've found you and this time I'm not going to let you fly off again."

"Oh — I don't *want* to. What good fortune that life is giving us a second chance, but darling, there's Margaret."

"Yeah — yeah, don't worry, I'll work that out. Now that you know the ranch and like it . . ."

"I love it!"

"Great, well, what do you say to leaving New York and coming to stay here? You can do some writing whilst I'm at the Clinic, and I'll be up every week-end until I can manage to get a divorce, then we'll be married and be constantly together."

During the next week they all went riding, fishing, swimming, walking and they would return to the Ranch tired and hungry, then they showered, changed, dined, watched a little TV, played cards or sat reading.

One evening Karyn stood up telling herself she should give Grans and Doc a break and let them alone. "Well I'm going to hit the sack," she said.

She kissed Joan's cheek, then David's, "Nite Doc." Warmed by the benign expression in his blue eyes, she suddenly added, "I can't go on calling you Doc, so may I call you D.D., it's short for Darling Doc?"

"Karyn honey," a smile spread over his long bony face, "that's just what I'd like."

"I like it too." Joan was delighted with Karyn's affection for David. "Well, I'll also say goodnight D.D.!"

She longed to remain but would not risk arousing the slightest suspicions in Karyn about her relationship with him.

It was Joan and Karyn's final day on the ranch. As they were about to leave for the airport Roy telephoned from Scotland.

"Nugget honey, we're definitely flying out tomorrow for New York, thank God. When do you get there?"

"Our 'plane leaves in an hour — I can't wait to see you."

"You can say that again, I'll call you the instant I get in. I *love* you."

"And I love you . . ." she whispered into the 'phone then hung up. Oh Lord! Here was that awful giddy feeling again, but she must not faint! She must not! But there was whoozing in her ears, salt in her mouth, then everything went black.

Joan and David found the white-faced girl in a heap on the tiles. David scooped her up in his arms and carried her to bed.

"Whatever is the matter?" Joan cried.

"Excitement I should think," David said, as he held spirits of ammonia to Karyn's nostrils whilst Joan unhooked her bra.

A minute later Karyn's eyelids fluttered open. "Oh Lord!" she murmured, "How crazy . . . I passed out again."

"Yes and, young lady, when you're in New York you go to your doctor — without delay. Maybe you're anaemic or something, but he must find out about these fainting fits."

"Yes, D.D., I promise, I'll go to see Doc Turner."

"Good. Now, when you feel up to it we'd better be on our way."

The first moment that Joan was out of Karyn's hearing she told David, "I'm worried about her. What causes these fainting fits do you think?"

"Fainting is a temporary lack of blood supply to the brain, caused by a number of things, but with Karyn I'd say her emotions are responsible. Anyhow, have your doctor check up on her."

Thirteen

"You both look wonderful," Moira said. "The vacation has been good for you. Let's have a drink then tell me everything. What's the ranch like?"

In the living-room Joan sank into her favourite chair. "The ranch is simply bliss, the house is old Spanish style with lots of charm, and the land is heavenly."

"Great! And I guess Doctor Murdoch was heavenly too?" Moira teased.

"I've fallen for him, Mother," Karyn burst out, "and I've a hunch he's *crazy* about Grans."

"Hurrah!" Moira cried. "Wowie — what a love story." She handed Joan a Scotch-on-the-rocks and turned to Karyn, "And how about your romance, sugar?"

"Roy gets in tomorrow! I just can't wait, but now I've gotta go shampoo my hair." She rushed away and Joan and Moira laughed at each other across the room. Joan was greatly tempted to tell her daughter, whom she knew longed for her to be happy, about the marvellous understanding she and David had reached, but she decided it was unlucky to talk of one's hopes too far in advance of them materializing.

"But you only had ten days at Cape Cod," she said. Joan's eyes studied Moira's beautiful face for signs of fatigue but happily there were none. "Was that enough of a break for you, darling?"

"Oh yes, it was business mixed with pleasure, I had several artists in the cast of the little Theatre, but I enjoyed myself, there were plenty of friends around and Rocky has been in and out of town which gave me a great lift. Tell me, did Karyn have any dates out there?"

"No, it was all very quiet."

"But she wasn't mooning over Roy, I hope, because he mightn't be so keen after two months absence — you know he's pretty young."

"Oh, but he 'phoned every day which kept her content, then she had loads of outdoor sports, she's in good shape, excepting she fainted twice. David said it's nothing to worry about but I'll make a date for her to see Doctor Turner tomorrow for a checkup."

"Fine, I guess she's still growing; maybe that's it." The bell on the oven started to ping and Moira jumped up. "Dinner will be ready in fifteen minutes — okay?"

The next afternoon Roy telephoned from Kennedy Airport to tell Karyn he was not driving home with the family but taking a cab directly to her apartment. Terribly excited, she rushed to the living-room to plump up the cushions thinking, Swell of Grans to have gone out so I can greet Viking alone! Then she went to watch at the window hoping to spot his cab draw up and soon afterwards the bell rang and she dashed across the living-room to the corridor, released the three locks on the hall door and flung it wide open. The next second she was wrapped in Roy's arms, the breath being crushed out of her. He was kissing her all over her face, her eyes, her nose, her mouth.

"Oh, Nugget! Is it good to see you? My wonderful little Nugget — God, how I missed you!"

She led him by the hand to the living-room. "Viking darling, how English you look, in your pin-striped suit."

"Yes, this was mother's idea to deck Nicky and me up as English gentlemen — we had to spend hours at the tailor in Savile Row."

"You look swell — super — colossal and I love-love-love you."

"I didn't know how much I loved you until the bloody Pond separated us. I'll *never* leave you so far away again, but sit down, I've something for you."

They settled side by side on the couch, he dug into his jacket pocket and pulled out a small velvet box which he put in her hand. "Open it, darling. Cartiers in Paris made it from my design, for you."

Her heart still thumping from the excitement of his being there, her thumb pressed the spring on the box, the lid flew up and she gazed with delight at a ring made of small gold hearts with a ruby in the centre of each.

"Oh, how lovely — lovely," her voice came in gasps. "It's *the* loveliest ring I've ever seen."

"An eternity ring, darling. Let's see how it fits." He slipped it onto the little finger of her left hand. "Is it too big, honey?"

"No, no! It's perfect, absolutely perfect — I just *love* it, Viking!" She gazed at him with adoring eyes.

He grinned widely. "Next one will be an engagement ring — then a wedding ring — until then, this one is my band of ownership."

"You don't need a visible band, darling — all of me belongs to you."

"I guess I really know that, honey. Now, about tomorrow, shall we spend the day at the cottage in Westchester? We won't be disturbed because I reckon Nicky and Claudine will be sleeping off the jet lag."

"Oh yes — the whole day alone!" She held her hand up to kiss her ring. "I'll never love another present as much as this one."

"Great! Well, darling I'll make tracks for home, change out of this get-up, then pick you up at seven and we'll go on the town."

In the 'Great American Steakhouse' in the Village, Roy steered Karyn over to a table where Nicky and Lynda were waiting for them.

"Hi, honey!" Nicky planted a kiss on Karyn's cheek as he caught her in a bear hug.

"Hi, Punk," Roy laughed, "she's my girl, remember?"

"Sure, sure," Nicky laughed, letting go of Karyn, and she and Lynda kissed.

"Hi, Karyn, long time no see."

"Yeah, I was on a ranch in California."

"And I went to Japan with my Dad. But isn't it great to have these two guys back again?"

"Oh, isn't it just," Karyn smiled widely into Roy's face as, beneath the table, he squeezed her knee.

"Crikey, it's good to be back, although in

some ways it was a wonderful trip, but this guy," Nicky nodded toward Roy, "went around like a Zombie. He looked at all the wonders but couldn't wait to get away to 'phone this little temptress." He winked at Karyn.

"And what about you, Nicky?" Lynda pouted. "Did you miss me? I didn't get eye-strain reading your postcards."

"Aw, baby, I'm the strong silent type from Marlboro country, but how about drinks?" He called the waiter and gave everyone's order.

"I thought you'd forgotten all about me," Lynda said teasingly.

"Not likely, baby, but the competition was tough."

"Aw, don't believe him, Lynda," Roy placated her. "Anyhow, we didn't stay anywhere long enough for the crazy guy to get involved. Mother had us moving so fast it was like being on a conveyor belt."

"Yeah, Claudine 'phoned me today," Karyn told Lynda, "and she said the two months was like two years — and she was lucky enough to have Carl join her."

The drinks arrived and they toasted each other. "Carl and Claudine aren't coming tonight," Roy told them. "His parents wanted him and Claudine to dine at their place."

"Was Carl able to keep her off the grass?" Lynda asked.

"Not quite 'off' it, but he made her cut down." Nicky looked frowningly at Roy. "I get worried about her."

"It beats me why she wants it so much," Lynda said. "She's not from a broken home like I am, she's got everything, as well as the guy she wants. What's eating her?"

Roy shrugged wide shoulders, "God knows, she may ease up now that we're home. I think she had too much of 'Mother'! But let's order."

They studied the big menus. "I know what I want," Roy said. "Cracked crab, then the biggest, honest-to-God T-bone steak in America. I'm all through with fancy sauces for a time."

"Right, man, I'll have the same," Nicky said, then the girls decided to follow the brothers' choice. "Okay," Roy said, "and we'll drink champagne to celebrate our homecoming."

Fourteen

The following morning before Roy and Karyn left for Westchester, Joan insisted that Karyn must keep a ten o'clock appointment which Joan had made for her at Doctor Turner's surgery, so Roy drove her there.

Whilst Karyn was with the doctor, he sat in the waiting-room, one long leg resting over the other hoping Karyn's fainting spells meant nothing more than anaemia which was easily cared for. Then he heard the door to the doctor's office open; Karyn had come out. How lovely she looked in her wide-skirted flowered dress, the neckline cut off the shoulders, her hair . . . but her huge eyes were loaded with distress! Christ! What dreadful diagnosis had the Doctor made?

He strode toward her, caught her elbow and wordlessly walked her out of the waiting-room. In the corridor he stopped.

"Darling, what the hell is wrong?"

"A baby . . . oh Viking . . . a baby." Her great eyes were round with anguish.

"A baby! You mean you're going to *have* one!"

She nodded and tears splashed out. "Yes

119

— oh, I took the pill on the second time we were together — so it must have happened on the very first day!"

He felt a bit shaken, "A baby! Whew! Christ, you had me all het up, I thought you had cancer or something fatal."

"I'm sorry about the baby, Roy . . . because . . . you see nothing on earth could make me have an abortion — not even to please you. I'd never kill . . ."

"For Christ's sake, forget it!" Alone in the corridor he caught her in his arms, crushing her to himself. "I'd never *let* you have a bloody abortion! Are you crazy! We'll be married at once — it's all quite simple."

She laid her cheek against his chest as relieved sobs burst from her. Momentarily she had feared he might be furious at the news, now she felt guilty at having so misjudged him.

"Your mother — she'll hate it," she murmured.

"To hell with that, she's got nothing to do with it. You're *my* Nugget!"

"But, darling, you've got to finish at Harvard, but if you marry me your father might refuse to pay your fees."

"Who cares? I've a fortune coming to me from my grandfather's trust — when I'm twenty-five. Five million bucks! Any moneylender will go wild to finance me! We'll get a home near Harvard and we'll all be together, you as my wife with my son, the three of us!"

"Oh, darling Viking, — would you be sorry to have a girl?"

"We'll send a girl back of course. God, how I love you." He started to dry her eyes with his handkerchief. "Come on, let's get out to the cottage where we'll be at peace to make our plans."

"Oh yes, yes," her wide smile was radiant, "but I must run back to tell Doctor Turner I'm going to be married and he must be sure not to let my family know I'm pregnant."

"Right — later we can pretend it's a seven-month baby."

"Oh Viking — how clever of you." She started to dash to the Doctor's door, but he warned, "Take it easy, sugar, you have two to think of now."

They lay on the big bed, arms around each other, her head on his chest. For these first few minutes after lovemaking they both felt too emotional to talk. Then he put his big hand gently on her flat stomach as if in a benediction.

"Hard to believe that you've really got our child curled up in this flat little belly."

"I'm flat now, thank goodness, and I'm

glad, so no one can guess about the baby, but after we've married I'll be proud as a peacock when my tummy grows huge. I'll want the whole world to know that I'm carrying Viking's baby."

"I'll have a T shirt made for you with the words painted it, 'Viking's baby' and an arrow pointing to your swollen tummy. You know, I think our son's going to be a world famous scientist."

"Oh, I hope I have a little boy just like you. What shall we call him?"

His hand smoothed gently over her satiny skinned body. "Well, I guess I haven't got a favourite male name. Of course it would be nice to please Father and give our child a family name. How do you like Cornelius or Christian, they've featured strongly in the Van Buren line."

"I *love* Christian Van Buren. Oh yes, it's super, and if by some chance it's a girl, we'll call her Christina Van Buren."

"Well, honey — that was easy, wasn't it? Hope we have such luck naming our other three kids."

"Three? Is that what you want, a family of four?"

"Yeah, four's a good number, I reckon, how about you?"

"Sure, it's a bit lonely being an only child.

Sometimes I almost envy you having Nicky and Claudine — and your three kid sisters as well."

"From now on they'll be your sisters and Nicky your brother too. Say, sugar, we'll need Wasserman tests, before we can marry, we'll ask Doc Turner to do them. Tomorrow I guess I'll drive up to our place in Newport to tell Mother and Dad — they left for Newport today; she can't take the heat in New York."

Karyn felt uneasy about this but only said, "Okay darling."

"I'll get a special licence in New Jersey, I think that's best — the Van Buren name shouldn't attract the Press there — we don't want a crowd around gaping at us."

"Darling, I hope you won't have to tell your parents about the baby but I don't mind Claudine and Nicky knowing."

"I'll try not to tell my parents — but if they ask why the rush to marry, I've got to give some explanation."

"I hate your mother having to know. She's all set against me as it is — this will make things worse."

"Forget it, sweetie. You can bet on it that she'll never tell anyone that her eldest son made such a slip."

She raised herself on an elbow to look

down into his beloved face. "Dear God, I pray they'll be glad to have a grandchild."

"Quit worrying, leave it all to me, but you'd better tell your family we're getting married at once because I want to take you back to Harvard when I go."

He reached down to kiss her breast. "Lucky baby, he's going to be able to suck those lovely nipples just whenever he's hungry." He suddenly frowned anxiously. "You *do* want to breast-feed him, don't you? You know it's much better for the baby."

"Of *course* I do! Viking, do you doubt it for a moment? I want to be the best wife and mother in the whole world."

Fifteen

When Karyn got home she knocked on Joan's door, "Grans, may I come in?"

"Yes, yes, darling." Joan was in bed reading, she put her book down then turned to Karyn, "Well! You look like the pussy cat that's swallowed all the cream." Joan thought the girl's beauty was growing daily.

"I've the most marvellous news! I'm going to be *married* next week!"

"*What* good news darling, I'm delighted!" Then, hating herself for the sudden suspicion that sprang to her mind, Joan asked, "But why so soon?"

"Because Roy wants me to go with him when he returns to Harvard. I can't wait to tell Mother — hey, that's her key in the lock." She bounded into the hall, threw her arms around the surprised Moira and pulled her into Joan's bedroom crying, "Roy and I are going to be married!"

"Darling baby!" Moira felt weak-kneed with happiness. God, what a break for Karyn to marry a Van Buren! She looked at Joan, "Isn't it absolutely super?" she laughed delightedly, "as Mother of the bride I've got to give the reception. Whew! A big society wedding! What will that set us back?"

"Mother! Wait, it's not going to be a big society wedding. We're going to be married without any fuss, very quietly next week so that I can go with Roy when he leaves for Harvard."

Moira sank onto the side of Joan's bed, "But, what a shame to sort of sneak off to be married, you'd look so gorgeous in a bride's get-up. I'll bet Roy's mother won't go for a quiet affair."

"She'll have to; he's determined there won't be any fuss. He's driving up to Newport tomorrow to tell his parents about our marriage, then he'll come in to talk to you and Grans."

Joan jumped out of bed. "Come on, we're going to open up a bottle of David's pink champagne and celebrate the wonderful news."

In the living-room Joan and Moira toasted Karyn then they all sipped their champagne.

"I'm so happy, happy — happy!" Karyn cried, doing a couple of ballet turns around the room. "I could really take off and fly — oh! . . ." She suddenly stood still, "I feel so sick . . ." Hand clamped over her mouth, she rushed out of the room.

From the bathroom came the sounds of

Karyn retching, which made Moira and Joan exchange knowing looks, then Moira muttered, "Do you think that . . . ?"

"Yes." Joan gave a nod. "I'm afraid so. Fainting twice on the Ranch, now retching and the hasty marriage — it all adds up, I suppose Doctor Turner told her this morning."

A little shocked, Moira sank onto a chair. "Oh, praise God, Roy's such a fine man! Just supposing he didn't want to marry the poor little thing?"

A great weariness started to creep through Joan. Ridiculous, she knew, but she would have sworn on all she held sacred that with Karyn's religious beliefs she would never have let Roy make love to her. But she had, and in a strange way it saddened Joan. She said, "I think it would be better to pretend we suspect nothing."

Roy swung the red Porsche into a private driveway of the Van Buren estate. "This is going to be no clambake, man." He threw the words at Nicky. "I'll say 'Hallelujah' when we're out of here tonight and headed back to New York."

"Don't let it get you down. You know damn well that Mother's going to act up. She'll fight your marriage like a stuck pig and she'll zoom in on the 'rush' wedding. She'll demand to know why."

"Well, to hell with that — Karyn doesn't want her to know about the baby."

The car was approaching a massive mock Georgian house of dazzling white where Roy pulled up, and the brothers got out and ran up a shallow flight of wide marble steps. Before they reached the hall door it swung silently open and an English butler, in 'morning suit', greeted them. Mrs Van Buren employed only English staff at all the family establishments.

"Good day, gentlemen, Doctor and Mrs Van Buren have just finished lunch, they're taking coffee on the terrace. May I send for your bags?"

"Thanks Williams," Nicky said, "but we're not staying the night. We'll go join our parents with coffee. No need for you to announce us."

The butler bowed, "As you wish, sir."

They crossed the large flagged hall, strode down a wide corridor and out onto a broad marble terrace. Ann Van Buren immediately caught sight of the brothers and, with delight, rose swiftly from her wicker chaise longue, her pale, aristocratic face almost lively with smiles.

"Just look, Peter!" She called to her husband who was dozing in a chair beside her. "Our wonderful sons are here." At arm's-length she held out hands to Roy and Nicky. Her figure was dagger thin in a white cotton gown, her golden hair was caught up with a ribbon and pinned atop her head.

'She's on stage, as usual', Roy thought cryptically as he dutifully clasped one of her hands and kissed her cheek, then Nicky did the same.

"You're looking great, Mother, quite recovered from the jet-lag," Roy said.

"Oh, not yet, darling — you know with my delicate health, it will take time." She sank back to lie on her wicker chaise longue.

Peter Van Buren shook hands with his sons. "Well, well, what a nice surprise," he smiled, "but we only parted two days ago, what's happened? Have you found you can't get along without us?" He sat down again on an upright chair.

"That's about it, Father." Roy forced a little laugh as he sat between his parents, with Nicky sitting opposite completing the circle.

Following the plan of action that the brothers had decided upon on the journey down, Nicky now opened up the conversation. "Roy's come to give you great news —

I just came along for the ride."

"Oh, and what is this great news?" Ann instinctively felt on the defensive.

"I'm going to be married," Roy said quietly, whilst every nerve in his body felt rigid.

"Married!" Ann gasped, her eyes seeming to protrude from their sockets.

"And whom do you intend to marry?" Van Buren asked coldly, offended by Roy's detached manner of announcing the news.

"Karyn Kirbo, Dad."

"Karyn Kirbo!" Ann exploded. During the trip she had arranged to censor all the family mail. Roy had received no letters so Ann had convinced herself he had broken with this girl. "You don't truly intend to marry that girl from the notorious family?"

"What's notorious about the family?" Though furious, Roy spoke coolly, "Or maybe you mean 'famous' Mother?"

"I'm quite aware of the difference between famous and notorious, and I mean *notorious* — which means unfavourably known."

"Then you're mistaken, Mother, the family consists of three women, grandmother, mother and Karyn — they don't smoke cigarettes or pot, they're not lushes. They are hard-working, decent people."

"You're talking like a half-wit! The girl's father . . ."

"Her name is *Karyn,* Mother," Nicky interrupted. "She's a damn fine girl, I just wish that she were twins so I could have a girl like her."

"Nicholas, kindly don't interrupt your mother," Peter Van Buren ordered.

"Oh, sure — sure, I was just trying to help."

"Thank you," Ann spoke icily. "To continue, the man committed suicide — not only because he'd lost his money, but because his wife was so promiscuous, playing around all over Hollywood, that he . . ."

"That's a dirty lie, I'll bet!" Roy exclaimed. "And anyhow, why is Karyn saddled with her parents' sins?"

"Right, my boy, she shouldn't be." Van Buren used a conciliatory tone, "But with her parents' doubtful behaviour as an example what kind of wife do you expect her to make?"

"A *marvellous* wife, Dad! She's got the best nature I've ever known. She's all I want for a wife."

"The whole idea is impossible!" Ann cried, feeling her heart burst from her body. "That you, a Van Buren heir, should marry such a nobody. Oh, now you imagine you're in love with her, but you must get over it. Then, later, when you're in your thirties

131

you'll marry a girl from a fine American or European family."

Roy had to control his temper, to hell with her arranging his life. "Sorry, Mother, but I'm *going* to marry Karyn next week and I'm taking her to live with me near Harvard."

"Good God, you're crazy!" Peter sprang to his feet. "You're going into your second year of Medical and you intend to saddle yourself with a wife! Get engaged to Karyn if you insist, then marry when you've got your degree. If she loves you so much she won't mind waiting for you."

"I don't want to do it that way, Dad. I want to marry at once — I'm happy having Karyn with me."

"But *why* such extraordinary haste?" Peter's dark eyes appealed to Nicky, "Talk some sense into him — make him wait."

"Dad, it's Roy's life — and I reckon he can marry and study at the same time. Thousands of students are doing it."

"Oh God!" Ann burst out as suddenly enlightenment struck her, "She's *tricked* you! She claims she's pregnant! She's appealed to your sense of decency! Oh, you poor, poor fool. You intend to be chivalrous and marry her."

"You're all wrong — all wrong," Roy beat

his clenched fists on his knees.

"If she is pregnant we'll arrange for her to have an abortion." Ann threw a desperate glance at her husband who nodded, and she went on, "But for God's sake, my darling Roy, don't ruin your life by marrying her. Don't you see? She's a little schemer, after the Van Buren fortune!"

Roy jumped up, his blue eyes blazing with fury. "Of all the dirty, rotten things you've said — that beats the lot." He stood, towering over Ann, his face so distorted with hate that Nicky sprang to his feet.

"Steady on, mate. You must remember Mother doesn't know Karyn properly."

"And she never will — you can bet on that!" He turned toward his father. "Don't worry, Dad, my marriage won't disrupt my studies — I'll carry on at Harvard."

"Not on your Father's money — you won't!" Ann struggled out of her chair, "I'll see to it that you don't have a cent from him if you marry this tramp!"

"God damn you to Hell!" Roy slowly and deliberately uttered the curse, then strode away.

"I'm right with you fella," Nicky called after him, then tried swiftly to console his father, "Don't worry, the marriage will be okay."

He dashed through the house to the hall door; outside Roy was already in the driver's seat in the open Porsche. Nicky jumped over the passenger door and settled down, then Roy roared off.

Shaking with agitation, Ann ran through the house to a front window to watch her sons leave. She felt sick enough to collapse, but she would stop the marriage! Somehow — somehow! Her confused brain raced on, she would 'phone the girl — offer her $50,000 to give Roy up — warn her the family would fight the marriage. No, she would offer $100,000 to buy the girl off. Roy, her wonderful son, her arms ached to hold him, her breasts ached to crush him to them and never let him go to any other woman. She would not lose him — she would not . . .

As the Porsche sped down the driveway Nicky said, "Thank Christ the worst is over." He glanced sideways at Roy's grim profile, "Hi there man, don't be so uptight. Dad will try to talk Mother out of this bloody hate she has for Karyn."

"She's a first class bitch and I hate her! I didn't have to tell them I was gonna be married — Christ! What a nut I was to think I'd get their blessings. And, calling Karyn a tramp who's after the bloody dough. What's the matter with Father? Why does he let her get away with all her crap?"

"She's castrated him with her aristocratic beauty and noble blood line," Nicky was trying to be humourous to break down Roy's fury, "he should have taken her to a shrink years ago, but take it easy man, no need to burn up the bloody road! Want a snort? I've got some bourbon in my hip flask."

"Yeah — I need it." Roy took the silver flask from Nicky, put it to his lips, downed several long swallows and handed it back. "Shit! I'm trembling like a kitten chased by a Doberman."

"Want me to take the wheel?"

"Hell, no! Driving is a help!"

"Yeah, but cut the speed, sure this is a country road but there are other cars in the world."

"Oh fuck them! I'll . . ."

"Roy for Christ's sake! Look out!"

A car suddenly turned out of a side lane and came right at them. "The bloody fool's on the wrong side of the road!" Roy shouted.

He twisted the wheel to avoid the oncoming car but too late, the car caught the Porsche head on. There was a hellish sound of crunching metal and shattering glass as the brothers were flung out of the open Porsche onto the road. The driver of the other car was pinned behind the steering wheel — a heart attack had killed him before the collision.

Karyn and Joan sat in the living-room watching television but Karyn could not concentrate on the programme. Her mind was on Roy, wondering how his meeting was going with his parents.

At midnight Joan said, "Well, I've watched enough nonsense, I'm going to bed."

"Yeah, me too. Maybe Roy's spending the night at Newport and he'll 'phone me in the morning."

They kissed each other then went to bed.

Joan awoke earlier than usual, pulled her drapes wide to let the sun flood the room, then turned on the 7 A.M. news very low so as not to disturb Moira and Karyn. Seated at her dressing-table, brushing her hair, she listened with part attention to news of China, Russia, Afghanistan, Iran. Always the same — dissension everywhere. She leaned over to snap the radio off, when the announcer said, "Now to America. Yesterday evening, on the Newport road, there was a bad car crash. The two sons of

Doctor Peter Van Buren were seriously injured and are now in the Van Buren Clinic in New York. In California . . ."

"Oh God," Joan murmured, switching the radio off. 'Seriously injured?' How badly — how badly? She felt near fainting, then the 'phone rang and she managed to pick the receiver up, "Yes — yes."

"Joan, it's David — I've just heard the news on the radio."

"Oh, David — it's hell! She's asleep — she doesn't know yet."

"Things may not be too bad — I'll be on the next 'plane out, so I'll be with you in a few hours."

"Thank you — oh, thank you," but he had already hung up.

Oh God, how could she tell Karyn the dreadful news? But surely she should first phone the Van Buren Clinic to discover the extent of the boys' injuries. She swiftly found the number in the book, then dialled it. As an operator answered, she said softly into the 'phone to be sure that Karyn, next door, would not overhear.

"I'm a close friend of the Van Buren brothers, would you please tell me, are they seriously injured?"

"Sorry, we are not permitted to give out any information."

"But, couldn't you just tell me if . . ."

"Sorry, I'm under strict orders." Click went the telephone.

Joan sat clutching the receiver in her shaking hand.

Sixteen

In a dazed condition, Karyn sat in the cab, between her mother and grandmother, as it pulled up before the tall white building of the Van Buren Clinic, where the steps to the entrance were crowded with photographers and reporters.

"God! We'll have to barge through that mess," Moira muttered, as she and her mother got out of the taxi then helped Karyn out. Moira paid the driver and, grasping Karyn by one arm, whilst Joan took the other, they began to manoeuvre a way through the crush of Press people.

"Please let us by," Moira pleaded, "we've come to see a very sick person."

"At eight in the morning? Sounds like a terminal case," a reporter said.

"I know about that honey of a girl," a man cried. "One of the brothers is sweet on her." He pushed up to Karyn, "Say Miss, is your feller Roy or Nicky?"

Incapable of speech, Karyn's eyes stared from a marble-like face as click, click went the cameras, then Joan begged, "Please have a little pity! Let us through."

"Okay lady, but give us the story when you come out."

A path was opened for them and they hurried up and into the building, where Moira went to the desk where a white-clad receptionist waited.

"May we see Mr Roy Van Buren, please — I know we're very early."

"Are you a relative? Only relatives are allowed in now. Visiting hours are 2 to 4 and 6.30 to 8."

"But, as this has been an accident we thought that . . ."

"Are you a relative? You didn't answer me."

"No, I'm not, but my daughter is *Roy* Van Buren's fiancée."

The receptionist's bright eyes darted to Karyn. "Well, okay. They're on the fourth floor. You'll have to ask the nurse up there if you can see him. The elevators are just behind you."

On the fourth floor the nurse told them, "Mr Roy Van Buren is in intensive care; he hasn't regained consciousness since the accident."

"After all these hours?" Karyn gasped with dismay, clutching at her heart, "Is his life in danger?"

The nurse's sympathetic brown eyes fastened on to Karyn's distressed face. "I've not been told that, but he was badly concussed and he's still in a coma."

"Oh God!" Karyn groaned, burying her face in her hands as the nurse went on, "Mr Nicholas Van Buren's left arm was broken, but it's been set and he's sleeping comfortably. Come back at 2.30, the regular visiting hours — you could see Nicholas Van Buren then."

"But not *Roy* — not *Roy* Van Buren?" Karyn pleaded. "Couldn't I please see him, just for a moment — even if he's in a coma?"

"That's quite impossible — he's in intensive care."

At that moment Ann and Peter Van Buren, followed by Claudine, came out of Nicky's room, into the corridor. Seeing them, Karyn told Moira and Joan, "There are Roy's parents, I'll ask them to let me see him."

She moved swiftly down the marble floor to the Van Burens. Their faces were grey with anxiety, but the moment Ann's eyes landed on Karyn she straightened up like a soldier going into battle.

"Doctor Van Buren, please let me see Roy?" Karyn quickly begged, her eyes awash with tears.

"No! No! You shall not see him!" Ann

141

almost hissed as she grabbed Karyn's wrist in clawlike fingers. "You murderess! It's because of you that he's in this condition."

Staggered by the mad accusation, Karyn pulled her arm free. "How can you blame me? I wasn't even with him."

"Please don't worry, Karyn," Doctor Van Buren said. "My wife's distraught. She doesn't know what she is saying."

"I *do* know what I'm saying," Ann snapped viciously. "Roy was in such a state after our row about his marriage, he drove like a madman — that's why he's half dead now."

"Half dead!" Karyn cringed with agony.

"He *isn't* half dead, Karyn," Claudine burst out. "He's in a coma, but he can come out of it any moment. Isn't that true, Dad?"

"Most certainly that's what we're hoping for. He's on a breathing machine, Karyn, and a team of the best doctors are caring for him and — he was *not* responsible for the crash!" Van Buren sent a furious look at his wife. "The driver of the other car was dead — the car was out of control!"

"But, Roy? He will be all right — won't he?" Karyn begged piteously and the plea was echoed in Van Buren's heart. He gave a curt nod, "Yes — I believe so."

"And later, may I see him — please?"

"No!" Ann lashed out. "I'm going to give orders that you are not permitted in here."

"Keep quiet, Ann, for God's sake. Haven't we enough grief as it is?" Van Buren said wearily. "Come this evening, Karyn. Seeing you, more than anyone else, might help to bring him around."

"Oh, thank you, Doctor Van Buren!" Karen was ready to kiss his feet. "Shouldn't I stay — not wait until tonight?"

"No, no — go home and rest, you'll be more use to Roy and his doctors if you are calm — right now, poor girl, you're near hysteria."

"I'll do *just* what you say." She caught at his hand and kissed it, her warm tears falling onto his skin. Then, on shaking legs, she returned to Joan and Moira at the end of the corridor.

Watching her, Van Buren frowned then, turning to his wife he was shocked by the dangerous look in her eyes. "Don't you see, Ann? We *need* her," he said rapidly, "Karyn's voice might be the one to bring Roy around."

"That little tramp can never help my son! She's evil, with an evil influence."

"Go home, for Christ's sake, Ann." Peter turned to Claudine, "Take your mother home, make her rest. I'm going back into intensive care to confer with Roy's doctors."

"Sure, Dad," Claudine kissed his cheek warmly. She pitied him with all her heart, for with his medical knowledge he knew the truth about Roy — he could not indulge in the layman's optimism.

Moira cancelled all her appointments at her office to stay home with Karyn, and she and Joan told her all the comforting facts which they knew about recovery from coma.

"A coma is a very ordinary thing," Moira said, sipping some tea. "An overdose of drugs or poisoning, or a bang on the head can cause it. Cheer up, Karyn darling, when you go back this evening he'll probably be out of it."

"Oh, I pray so — how I pray so." Karyn sat upright in an armchair, twining her slim fingers in and out of each other.

Moira got up to look at the cup and saucer on the table beside Karyn's chair. "You haven't touched your tea. Do drink a little of it, darling, it will do you good."

Karyn slowly shook her head. "I can't, thanks Mother, I feel rather sick in my stomach."

At the sound of the hall door buzzer Moira put a hand on Karyn's shoulder, "Sit still, darling, I'll go."

"It might be David," Joan said hopefully and, seconds later, Moira was ushering him into the room.

At sight of him Karyn jumped up and flung herself into his arms. "Oh, D.D., thank God you've come." She felt that with his quiet strength he would be a help for Roy. "Roy's in a coma — but that's not fatal is it? Tell me — tell me."

He hugged her tightly, "Of course it's not fatal. Karyn, honey, I'm sure Roy's going to be okay." His look flew over Karyn's head to Joan, who stood watching him with big questioning eyes and tremulous mouth. He sent her a smile and unloosened his hold on Karyn, then settled her in the armchair. "Now then, sugar, tell me all you know."

She told him everything, ending with, "But the coma has lasted over twelve hours, doesn't that sound serious?"

"Not at all, but I can't say much about the whole thing until I've seen Doctor Van Buren. I'll take you to the Clinic when you're due at six. Say, Moira, how about a bourbon on the rocks for a weary traveller?"

"Of course, Doctor Murdoch." She went to the built-in little bar.

"The 'Doctor Murdoch' was fine when you were a small girl, now I'd like it if you

145

used Karyn's nickname for me, D.D. — stands for darling doctor —" he grinned, hoping to lift the tension in the room, "Nice eh?"

Moira was glad at the chance to smile. "*Very* nice, D.D., and will you stay with us instead of going to the Waldorf? We'd really like that — wouldn't we, Mother?" His strong male presence would be a help to all of them.

"Oh yes! Please *do* stay, David, we're rather a sad little trio of females — we need you."

"He can have my room, Mother, and I'll sleep with you," Moira said. "You *will* stay, won't you — please, D.D.?"

"Nothing I'd like more, if I won't be crowding you."

"Good, that's settled. I'll just get the ice." Moira left to go to the kitchen.

Joan sank back into her chair, as David sat on the couch taking out a cigarette. He was wondering just how deep Roy's coma was.

Karyn began to tidy the morning newspapers lying beside her chair as David said, "I saw the papers at the airport, but don't upset yourself by poring over them."

"Right, I won't, and I've got good news D.D. — Roy and I are going to be married!"

"That's absolutely great! When did this happen?"

"As soon as he got back we arranged it. He drove up to tell his parents about it . . . then, coming back, he had the crash."

David guessed at the state Roy's nerves must have been in after telling Ann Van Buren he intended to marry. That explained the crash. "Well, he'll be okay by the time the wedding comes along."

"Oh, I hope so, we planned to be married next week."

"Next week — that's pretty quick."

David shot an enquiring glance at Joan but she swiftly turned her eyes to Moira as she came in carrying the ice-bucket.

"Sorry I was so long but I had to answer the 'phone in the kitchen. It was C.B.S. news room wanting to speak to Karyn, of course I refused, then they asked, 'Is it true that she's engaged to marry Roy?' 'Yes,' I said, '*it is true!*' "

Moira had been most emphatic about confirming Karyn and Roy's engagement. After hearing from Karyn how Ann Van Buren had treated her at the Clinic, Moira had decided to broadcast Karyn's engagement, especially as she was probably pregnant. She handed David his bourbon on the rocks. "Hope that's okay, D.D."

"Thank you, Moira." He sipped the drink then asked Karyn, "What did your Doctor say about those fainting spells?"

Her face, the whole of her, visibly stiffened. She did not answer at once, she hated having to lie, then she said, "I'm anaemic but, of course, it's easily cared for."

Oh God, she suddenly felt so alone being unable to communicate with Roy and having to make her own decisions. Lying to the people who loved her, were suffering over her sorrow. Wanting to get away she stood up saying,

"Mother, I'll go and whip up a salad, shall I? It's getting near lunchtime."

"Do you feel up to it, darling?" Joan asked anxiously.

"Yeah — Grans, I want to *do* something — stops me thinking."

"Let's have a tuna salad," Moira suggested, "and, honey, don't answer the 'phone, I'll turn it on in here and we'll answer it." She switched on the button.

Karyn nodded and left, and Moira went on, "I guess we'll soon be inundated with calls when the engagement news come on the air, but all we have to do is give basic facts."

"I'd better go down and warn the doorman," said David standing up, "to watch out for reporters and stop them coming up."

"Oh, thank you," Joan said gratefully, and when he had left she said, "Praise God he's here, Moira, we'll need his help. If your suspicions are correct and she's pregnant . . ." Joan broke off as the telephone rang.

"I'll get it." Moira sprang towards the 'phone. "I guess the vultures have started."

For the next few hours the telephone rang constantly, with reporters calling from all over the country and to each one Moira strongly confirmed Karyn's engagement to Roy.

"Well, the engagement is being well and truly established," Moira told Joan with some satisfaction. "That Van Buren woman won't dare to deny it!" She was thinking, in a distracted way, that a legitimate engagement would be a help to Karyn if, God forbid, fate denied her a marriage to Roy.

Moira had just sat down when the telephone rang again. "Shall I leave it?" she wearily asked her mother. "All the important papers have the story already."

"No, no, let's answer it. Perhaps it's the Clinic to report on Roy!" Joan cried, "He might be conscious."

"God, yes." Moira grabbed the receiver. "Hullo."

"Hi Moira, sugar — that you? It's Rocky."

"Oh Rocky!" Her whole body relaxed at the sound of his strong voice, she was near tears.

"Say, honey, I've just heard about your kid's engagement, seen her on T.V., taken from a still shot. Christ, I'm sorry about the Van Buren boy."

"It's awful Rocky, he's been in a coma for more than eighteen hours."

"Hell, don't let it get you down, sugar, he might snap out of it at any moment. Anything I can do to help?"

Just talking to him instilled Moira with strength. "There's nothing you can do, thanks Rocky. I'm so glad you've called though."

"It bugs me to think of you being so upset. I'll fly in tomorrow. Can you dine with me?"

"Yes, yes. I don't see why not, Rocky."

"Great! I'll call you when I get in. 'Bye honey."

"Bye Rocky." Moira slowly replaced the receiver. How good it was that he cared so much about her troubles.

Seventeen

With an arm held protectively around Karyn's shoulders, David elbowed a way through photographers and reporters up the Clinic's steps. To all the questions hurled at Karyn about her engagement, he answered "No comment".

At the entrance a patrolman now stood guard and David told him, "I'm Doctor Murdoch with Miss Kirbo — we are expected."

"Yes, sir, come right on in."

Inside the receptionist said "Go up, please — fourth floor. Doctor Van Buren's there."

David thanked her and, moving to the elevator, he told Karyn, "Now don't go to pieces, honey, if Roy doesn't look quite like 'your' Roy. If you cry or demonstrate any weakness you won't be allowed to see him again for some time."

"Yes, yes, I'll be very calm."

Inside the waiting-room Doctor Van Buren came forward, nodding to Karyn he took David's hand.

"I appreciate your coming, Murdoch. I'll put you in the picture very quickly. We've

151

stabilized Roy's breathing, the team of Doctors was afraid of pneumonia so they performed a tracheotomy." His dark eyes burned into Karyn's eyes, "Don't be frightened when you see a hole in his windpipe with a plastic tube coming from it — that's pumping air from a respirator into his lungs."

Karyn found David's hand and grasped it tightly, "I'll be all right, Doctor Van Buren." In a desperate voice she pleaded, "Is Roy any better than this morning?"

"No change, let's go in."

Clinging to David's hand she followed Doctor Van Buren into the shadowy room. Oh God! Roy lay like a corpse stretched on the bed, his big body covered by a sheet.

"Talk to him, Karyn," Van Buren ordered in quiet urgency. "Touch him, call him! Do your *damndest* to get some response from him."

She bent her head down to his beloved face, "Roy darling, it's Karyn — Viking darling! It's Nugget — I love you — I love you, Viking, darling, *please* hear me — *please!*" She leant lower to tenderly kiss his moist cheek but no response came, not even the flicker of an eyelid, and that awful tube in his throat looked terrifying. "Roy — Roy!

Answer me — Viking! Darling, please ma.
a little sign." 'God be merciful', she prayec
'let him hear me.'

A hand on her shoulder pressed her to sit
on a chair. David said, "Just keep calling
him, honey — don't let up."

"I will — I will! I'll *make* him hear me!"
She leaned close to Roy's ear. "Viking, Viking! Please hear me, Roy darling. Roy! Roy!
It's Nugget — you *must* answer me, oh Roy,
please *hear* me! Roy . . . Ro . . . y!" It was
her heart crying to him. "Roy! Darling Viking!"

"No use," Doctor Van Buren sighed
heavily. "Absolutely no response."

"Let me stay here, I beg you, Doctor Van
Buren," Karyn pleaded. "Let me keep calling him — he will hear me — I know he
will!"

"Go on — go on for as long as you can,"
Van Buren muttered as he walked to the
bottom of the bed to join David. In a low
voice he asked, "Why does she call him Viking?"

"It's her nickname for him."

"Ah . . . I 'phoned Palmer this afternoon,
in Zurich. You know, he's one of the finest
neurologists in the world. He's flying back
from Switzerland, he'll be here in a few
hours. The lab. tests show no sign of drugs

153

in Roy's blood, besides Nicky swears he seldom touches 'grass'. We've done a brain scan but it's revealed nothing to help us. We're waiting for Palmer to arrive."

"Viking darling, you must answer me — please, please." Karyn continued her litany of love and, suddenly Roy jerked his head up with such force that the whole bed shook. "He's hearing me!" Karyn jumped joyously to her feet. "He is hearing me!"

"No, no, honey," David said gently, "that was just part of convulsions; sometimes it accompanies being in coma."

Now Roy's head started to roll from side to side on the pillow, as if he were fighting some kind of hidden restraint. Then deep groans came from his throat. Terrible, wild guttural sounds, that tore at Karyn's soul.

"He's in pain! Oh God! He's suffering!" She whispered desperately to David.

"I assure you he's not in pain, he cannot conceive pain in his mind so his body feels nothing at the moment. But I guess you've stayed long enough." He glanced across the bed at Van Buren who gave a little nod.

"Yes, better go now, Karyn, and come at ten in the morning. I'll keep my wife away until eleven — no sense in you two meeting. She'll be coming at 7.30 tonight." He

glanced at David, "Thank you for coming, Murdoch."

"I'm staying with Karyn's family, so call me if I can help, my friend. I'll bring Karyn tomorrow. Maybe things will take a turn for the better once Palmer's here — he's a wizard with this type of case."

Outside in the corridor Karyn stood with tears streaming down her face. Agony to see her young, strong lover of two days ago, now lying helpless — his mind God knew where. David stood beside her, his hand on her shoulder, then a nurse came up and said, "Mr Nicholas is the next room to your left if you wish to go in."

"Do you feel up to it, Karyn?" David said.

"Oh yes, I want to see him."

They found him propped up against pillows in bed, his left arm bandaged and in a sling. Under his thatch of golden hair his good-looking face burst into an ear-to-ear grin as he saw Karyn.

"Jesus, Karyn! Am I pleased to see you, honey — and you too, Doctor Murdoch."

Karyn bent to kiss his cheek. As he hugged her with his strong right arm, he thought, the poor kid's pale as death. What a helluva shock for her, especially now she's carrying Roy's kid. He said gently, "Roy's gonna be okay, honey."

"What a lucky so-and-so you are Nicky," David said, "coming out of that mess with only a broken arm."

Nicky frowned down at his arm in the sling. "Yeah, I guess so."

"The break in the elbow?" David asked.

"Yeah."

"Plenty of pain attached to that."

"And how, but the nurses keep me filled up with pain killers. They tell me the whole bloody Clinic is revolving around old Roy." His right hand reached out to take Karyn's hand. "Did he know you, honey?"

She grasped his hand tightly, "No, nothing . . . he understood . . . nothing."

"But, it's early days, you gotta be patient. He can snap out of the coma any minute. Anyhow, you gotta hold up your wedding until the best man has two good arms." He gave a playful wink, "Can't kiss all the bridesmaids with a busted arm."

"Nicky — you're great." Karyn swallowed a sob while she sensed that Roy had told Nicky about the baby, and she was glad.

"I'll be outta here before you can count ten," he said seriously. "Then I'll take care of things till Roy's on his feet." He was trying to get across to Karyn that he knew about the baby and would look out for her.

She guessed some of his thoughts and said, "You mustn't push things, Nicky."

"Right," Murdoch looked at his wristwatch, "Karyn, it's nearly 7.30, time we were leaving."

"Oh yes!" She quickly got to her feet and kissed Nicky's cheek. "I'll be in tomorrow morning."

When Karyn and David returned from the clinic her grief-stricken face appalled Joan and Moira as Karyn said, "He's like a half-dead person." She buried her face in her hands and started to sob.

"But he'll improve with time?" Joan turned desperate eyes on David. "Won't he?"

Christ! How could he comfort them without lying? "Yes, yes, I've told Karyn she's got to be patient."

"Poor, poor Roy, he doesn't even know me and it makes me feel so alone — so alone and so terribly afraid."

"But darling, why should you feel so alone and afraid when we are here?" Joan said.

"You're going to have a baby, aren't you Sugar?" David said gently, "I guessed that when you fainted at the ranch — tell us when it is due?"

"In about six and a half months." Karyn's choking voice came from behind the screen of hair covering her face. Then she jumped up. "Oh, Oh! I feel so sick." She dashed out of the living-room with Moira racing after her.

Eighteen

Around the table in the kitchen alcove, David, Joan, Moira and Karyn sat silently eating breakfast. None of them had slept well, despite the mild sedative David had administered to them after they had seen an evening paper the previous night with a caption 'Roy Van Buren's Fiancée' under a photo of Karyn taken on the steps of the Clinic.

Karyn had lain awake storming the heavens for Roy's swift release from the coma; Joan, too, had been praying for Roy's recovery, also for Karyn who had told them all of the child she carried; David had tossed around plagued by depression. He had been really counting on Joan's promise to come to the ranch soon for a lengthy stay, but now this mess up over Karyn would put paid to that — Joan would obviously remain in New York to help her family.

Sleep had evaded Moira, for her mind was filled with the fear of Karyn producing an illegitimate child. Terrible for Karyn and the baby and hell for herself. And, who would find the money for all of it, Karyn's delivery, then support of the child? There was only one way out of the mess — Karyn must have an abortion. Not ideal, but what choice was there?

Now, despite David's presence, Moira was determined to discuss the matter, to make Karyn face the unpleasant facts.

"You know, darling, I was going over this situation in my mind for most of the night and I feel you've got to be very brave and realize that Roy could — I say *could* be in a coma for months, and not be able to marry you before the child's birth," Moira's brown eyes looked compellingly into Karyn's distressed face, "and you surely don't want to have a child on your own. Of course, I'll help all I can, you know that, but things aren't so hot for me at the moment. I just want you to consider every angle of this whole thing."

"But, what can I do?" Karyn murmured in a bewildered way.

"You can have an abortion," Moira said gently but firmly.

"Never! Never! I'd die first! With all my heart I *want* Roy's baby! I know I couldn't stay here, but I could go off somewhere and work till the baby comes. Grans will come with me — won't you, Grans?"

"You know I will, my darling!"

"You can come to Aurora Ranch, honey," David said, "I'll take care of you and deliver the child, and you both can stay there for as long as you like."

"Oh, thank you, D.D." Karyn's misty eyes bathed him in gratitude.

"All right," Moira murmured, "that would be a great help to begin with." She sipped her coffee, wondering if the Van Buren family would offer financial support for Karyn and the baby if Roy did not recover. But, time to think of that later.

Moira left then for her office and David and Karyn left to go to the Clinic. Feeling emotionally drained, Joan went to her room and lay down, and immediately she started to doze. The irritating sound of the internal buzzer awoke her and she went to the kitchen to answer it. "Yes?" she said into the earpiece connected with the downstairs hall.

"There's a Mrs Van Buren to see you, Ma'am," came the doorman's voice.

"Please tell her my grand-daughter's gone to the Clinic."

"I did, but it's *you* she wants to see."

It must be Claudine, Roy's sister. "All right, let her come up, please." Joan replaced the receiver thinking, Poor Claudine probably wants to talk about Roy's condition.

When the hall door bell rang she went to open the door, but it was not the seventeen year old Claudine, but a tall, elegant woman.

Joan swiftly said, "I'm sorry, you must have the wrong apartment."

"You *are* Mrs Clements?"

"Yes, I am."

"Then it is you whom I wish to see." A cultured, haughty English voice, accustomed to being obeyed. "I am Mrs Peter Van Buren, Roy's mother."

The woman who yesterday had been so brutal to Karyn, what did she want here? "Well, come in, please," Joan said coldly.

Ann Van Buren stepped inside, Joan swiftly shut and locked the door, then led the way to the living-room.

"Sit down, Mrs Van Buren. I simply can't imagine why you've called upon me."

Ann slowly looked around, then decided on a chair with its back to the window, as Joan settled in her favourite chair opposite her.

"I've called upon you because we must discuss important matters. We are country-women I believe," Ann said with a shadow of condescension."

"Not actually. I am of Irish descent."

"No matter, we must talk about Roy."

"I'm deeply sorry about his condition, but

162

one thing you needn't worry about is the strength of Karyn's love for him — she'd wait years, if necessary, for him to regain his . . ."

"That's just it!" Mrs Van Buren interrupted. "I've come to tell you that she must not attempt to hold onto Roy!"

Joan drew back as if iced water had been splashed onto her face. She spluttered, "I . . . I don't understand what you mean."

"It's perfectly simple, she must not try to hold onto Roy."

"But they're in love . . . engaged to be married."

"Rubbish! Absurd! The engagement means nothing. They'll *never* marry!"

Recovering a little from her first shock, Joan demanded, "What do you mean? He asked her to marry him, she's accepted. In the name of God, why are you trying to upset this?"

"Because she's utterly unsuitable as a wife for Roy!" Ann leaned forward in her chair, her thin pale face with its malevolent look seemed threatening to Joan. "My son is *not* going to marry her, I told him I'd never permit it the night of the crash — I warned him that she would pretend to be pregnant to trap him into marriage."

Enraged, Joan jumped to her feet. "How

dare you! My grand-daughter *is not* trying to trap your son! Unfortunately, she is pregnant by him and there's no pretence about it, and let me assure you that any man who wins her for a wife is *very lucky*."

"*Any* man who wins her — might be lucky, but *my* son is not *any* man. When he marries, I will help choose his wife. She must come from one of America's finest families, or nobility, — or royalty. On my side he stems from four generations of Earls, on the Van Buren side . . .'"

"You talk as if you were living two hundred years ago, but allow me to tell you that Karyn is well born. Her Irish ancestors are . . .'"

"Her present background is deplorable," Ann interrupted. "But in spite of that, I've come here to offer you and your grand-daughter $100,000 to drop this disgusting Press bombardment about being engaged to Roy. $100,000, but your grand-daughter must have an abortion — that is, *if* she is really pregnant."

The whole affair was like a frightful night-mare to Joan. "Mrs Van Buren, I *insist* that you leave!" she said decisively.

"Don't be so foolish, a hundred thousand dollars is not to be picked up so easily with one of your historical novels, so I advise you to accept my offer."

"You devil! There are things that money cannot buy, but you're too insane to know this. Now go! For God's sake *go!*"

Ann's eyes narrowed dangerously. "I'm warning you that I'll issue a statement to the Press denying that Roy is engaged to your grand-daughter — I'll make such a fool of her."

"And I warn you not to cast any rotten aspersions on Karyn. If you *do*, I'll tell the Press you're a psycho with an Oedipus complex — a filthy, incestuous mother in love with her sons." Joan had heard this from David and, without compunction, fought Ann with the knowledge. "That you offered me $100,000 to break Roy's engagement!"

Ann winced as if she had been struck. "You're a disgusting woman! How dare you try to distort a mother's noble love!" She rose to her feet. "You're also a fool to refuse my $100,000. I'll give . . ."

"Go away! Leave!" Joan waved furiously towards the door, and Ann swept out to the hall door, which Joan unlocked and threw open.

Ann hesitated before leaving, "I'll raise my offer to $125,000 . . ."

"Go to hell!" Joan gave her a furious push into the hall and slammed the door.

Hours later, Karyn and David returned from the Clinic, and David said, "This business takes a lot out of you. Go and lie down Karyn."

When Karyn had left Joan told David about Ann Van Buren's call. He was flamingly indignant.

"By God! That woman is a number-one bitch. I'll talk to Peter Van Buren about her; he must deal with her." Suddenly he grinned widely in a way Joan had always loved. "Say, honey, I'm glad you gave her a sample of your wild Irish temper. I was wondering if you'd lost it completely. I've not seen any of it for twenty-five years."

She could not help giving a little laugh. "Oh, it's still there when I'm faced with injustice and, darling, I had to protect Karyn from her. I only hope my threat of going to the Press has frightened her enough to stop her denying the engagement."

"Although she's insane enough to do anything, I still believe your threat will work. She'll do everything to avoid a scandal."

Nineteen

Peter Van Buren paced the floor of his spacious library, trying to ease his agitation. His mind was in torment — Palmer, the celebrated neurologist, could not fathom the extent of the damage to Roy's brain — no one knew what the outcome would be. And now, God damn it, Peter swore to himself, he must stop his neurotic wife from creating a scandal!

After hearing David's story about Ann's threat to Joan, Peter decided to summon Claudine to his aid for his confrontation with Ann.

Ann swept into the library, wearing her own peculiar draperies as if she were a nineteenth-century Duchess. "Peter, — oh, and you're here too, Claudine. *Well,* what is this meeting about?"

When Ann was seated, Peter began, "I've just learned, Ann, that you've told Karyn's grandmother that you intend to call the Press and deny Roy's engagement to Karyn. In God's name, why?"

"Because the whole thing is a lie! Roy never asked that tramp to marry him! It's her family's machinations to try to trap him. They have no proof of anything, and I'm going to publicly deny it!"

"You're mad, Ann! That girl is most important to Roy, the sound of *her* voice — *her* presence could well be the one thing that penetrates his brain. Damn you! Are you going to deprive him of that?"

Claudine longed to shake Ann, "Mother I was with Roy when he asked Karyn to marry him!" She disliked lying, but her mother's madness must be curbed.

"*Were* you, Claudine?" Ann laughed sarcastically, "You know I think you're lying to spite me. You've always been jealous of your brother's love for me. Next thing is that you'll claim she's carrying Roy's child."

"She is!" Claudine cried, knowing the truth from Nicky. "I was at school with Karyn for years and I swear she's the opposite of a tramp. She was a virgin until she slept with Roy, and if you harm her whilst Roy's unconscious he'll hate your guts when he comes round."

Peter grasped at this. "Claudine's right, he will hate you! I'm warning you, Ann, leave *Karyn alone!* Consider her as an instrument to help restore Roy's mind to us!"

"Yes, yes," she murmured, shutting her eyes, "my wonderful son."

"So, you promise, Ann, you won't ever contact a newspaper to deny the engagement?" Peter caught at her shoulders.

"Remember, Mother," Claudine burst out, "if you hurt Karyn, and her family sues you and subpoenas me, I'll have to tell the truth! I'll have to admit I heard Roy propose marriage to her."

"You see, Ann," Peter looked fiercely into her face, "you wouldn't have a leg to stand on, so promise me you'll never talk to the Press — or you'll be damaging Roy's name."

"But, Peter, never would I hurt my wonderful son — you know that he and Nicky are more to me than the air I breathe. I promise I won't talk to any newspaper people." Ah, but she would find some other means of freeing Roy from this girl — once Roy was again conscious. "Now, I'll go back and rest."

"Good, my dear." Peter opened the door for her. When she had left, he told Claudine, "Thank you, my dear daughter — it was you who made her realize the stupidity of her threats. Christ, what chaos life has become."

"Poor old Dad," Claudine went and put her arms around his neck, "it's a helluva time, but it's gotta work out okay."

"Yes, yes, now I'm going back to the Clinic, I'll see you there later."

Claudine went up to her bedroom, locked the door, slipped her shoes off and lay down with a lighted cigarette. She could hardly wait for the kind, friendly grass to take the sharp edge off her anxiety over Roy. Would he recover? He *had* to! Then he would marry Karyn and she would have the baby. Claudine pulled on the helpful cigarette as her mind meandered. Later, she and Carl would marry and they'd have a kid too. They'd all live together in some place far from New York . . . their lives would be great . . .

For the next six weeks Roy remained in a coma. Karyn's life was given over to four daily visits to him, each of a half hour's duration. Whilst she was seated beside Roy's bed she maintained a stream of talk to him, mentioning things they had done, places they loved, but never did he give a flicker of understanding.

Each time a visit of Karyn's ended she was replaced by Claudine or Nicky, for Nicky had decided not to return to Harvard until Roy recovered. Between them and Roy's parents, a constant rota was maintained so that at most times someone was orally trying to recall Roy's mind from its cruel captivity.

But Roy continued to lie with wide open

blue eyes, staring unseeingly at the ceiling. His body had shrunk, although he was fed intravenously. His face had fallen into hollows.

To Claudine, sitting beside his bed, it seemed a macabre race between Karyn's baby advancing along the road *into* life, and beloved Roy's retreating down the road *out* of life. Would he and his child ever meet? The sorrow of it all was sometimes so overwhelming that Claudine leaned more heavily on drugs. But, Karyn was far from despair. She believed that God would answer the beseeching prayers that she offered each morning at seven o'clock mass. So another four months plodded by.

Now, Doctor Turner, having completed Karyn's monthly check-up, looked across his desk at her and Joan seated opposite him.

"You've got to quit this self-inflicted martyrdom, quit spending so much time at the Clinic, it's bad for you."

"It's not martyrdom Doctor," Karyn querulously defended herself. "I go because I *must* be with Roy — one day I know my voice will get through to him."

"Yes, yes, but only *once* a day, no more of this business of *four* daily visits! Remember, it's not only Roy you have to consider,

171

there's his child too. In fact, the time has come when the child must come first. You've entered your eighth month but, considering all you've been through, it's possible you might not carry the full nine months. Another thing, you're hiding your condition too well."

"But I *have* to, Doctor! People mustn't know I'm pregnant until Roy recovers and we get married."

"Yes, yes, I understand the problem, but now I want your promise, Karyn, that you go to the Clinic only once a day."

"If you insist on that, Doctor." She felt cornered, how could she live seeing so little of Roy?

"I *do* insist. I'll go further and say I won't be responsible for you, or the child, unless you obey me." He frowned at her, "I don't suppose you want to lose your child?"

Karyn swallowed hard, "I'd die . . . if I did. But I won't — will I? Everything's all right now, isn't it?" Her frantic eyes beseeched him.

"Relax. Everything looks fine now, but just let's keep it that way. I suggest you make an evening visit to Roy. As it's cold weather you've an excuse to wear a full cloak to help conceal your figure; you must face the fact that next month you will not be able to visit

Roy at all because you'll be too obviously pregnant to keep the truth from the world . . ."

"Oh, but he will *recover* before then! He's *got* to!" Karyn cried frantically. "He would never let his child be born illegitimate. Somewhere, deep in his brain, he must know that." Suddenly tears were streaming down her pale cheeks as she sobbed, "He would never hurt me or his child, he *will* recover in time, I know it."

They said goodbye to Doctor Turner and took a taxi home. Karyn sat back against the upholstery and Joan heard the familiar whisper.

"Dear God, let him recover soon! Let him recover!" It became a continuous litany which Joan had become accustomed to hearing when alone with Karyn.

Joan was particularly agitated as, for time without number, she confronted a terrible thought that Roy would probably *not* recover in time to marry Karyn! So a home must be found for Karyn, herself and the baby! She must start apartment searching at once. David had offered them a permanent home on his ranch, but Karyn had begged to be allowed, after the birth, to live near Roy. Hard as it would be on their finances, an apartment must be found where they were unknown and, above all, where the Press would not unearth the secret that Karyn had borne an illegitimate child . . . *but she need not*. Suddenly the marvellous — saving idea flashed to Joan like lightning revealing a dark field. She knew exactly what she had to do — it was startlingly clear to her and, this very evening she would act upon it.

"I'll wake you in plenty of time to be ready for Nicky," she told Karyn as she tucked her into bed at their apartment.

When it was almost seven o'clock she went and opened the hall door and stood ready for Nicky, she didn't want the bell to awaken Karyn until everything was settled.

He arrived punctually and, putting a finger to her lips as a gesture for silence, she beckoned him to follow her into the living-room.

"Karyn's very tired after the visit to the Doctor, I thought we should let her sleep for a few more minutes."

"Sure, sure, there's no mad rush."

"Sit down, Nicky, have a drink."

"Thanks, I won't right now. Was the Doc's verdict okay on Karyn?"

"Well, he's terribly anxious about her and disapproves of the way she's trying to hide her condition; it's bad for the baby."

"Yeah, Claudine and I are worried about her too. This is a helluva time for her —

with Roy like this."

Joan sat beside him on the couch. "The Doctor fears the baby might come early so, if Roy is still in a coma, the child would be fatherless — *illegitimate!*" She grasped his arm, "Surely to God, you don't want your brother's child to be born illegitimate? A son, perhaps."

He stared at her in confusion, "Hell, no, *of course I don't want it,* but God only knows when Roy'll come out of the coma."

"That's just it! Nicky, loving Roy as deeply as you do, there's only one thing for you to do," she stared deeply into his confused looking eyes, "you must marry Karyn!"

"Christ Almighty!" He shook her hand off and sprang to his feet, his eyes blazing dangerously. "What a rotten idea! When Roy comes around he'll go berserk."

Joan jumped up to face him, "But it's only to *save* Karyn and the child from disgrace. You can *divorce her immediately!* Don't you see? The marriage won't be consummated — it won't be binding in any way! It's only so the child can be born a Van Buren, and Karyn can be protected. Surely Roy would want that for Karyn and his child."

He stared down at her with an angry frown but then with relief, she saw comprehension creeping into his eyes.

"You're damn right! Roy would want me to save them," he muttered slowly. "By Christ! I'll do it!"

"Thank God, Nicky," Joan murmured, feeling weak with relief.

"You're so damn right! I'm mad as hell with myself that *I* didn't think of it first! How dumb can I be — that you had to point it out to me."

"Don't worry about that, but you must pretend to Karyn that the idea is *yours*. Don't let her know I suggested it; she's so sensitive that she mightn't accept it."

"Sure — sure, but when shall we do it — the marriage, I mean?"

"We must see what Karyn wants, but I suppose she'll wait until the last moment hoping for Roy to recover. Oh Nicky, I'm so relieved we've fixed this up." She reached up and pulled his head down, kissing him on the cheek. "I'll go and wake her now — better not talk to her about the marriage idea tonight — she's really awfully tired — tomorrow, maybe."

"You're the boss Mrs Clements." Nicky gave her a little smile, inwardly he felt elated that he was to do something for Roy.

Twenty

Driving Karyn to the Clinic, Nicky's mind was filled with working out the practical method of marrying, then divorcing her, as secretly as possible.

Neither of them spoke much, and upon reaching the Clinic he accompanied her to Roy's room, then went to his father's private suite. Since the accident Van Buren spent most of his nights at the Clinic, to be on hand lest some change in Roy's condition required his aid.

Now Nicky gave a family knock of three taps on the living-room door and walked in, "Hi, Dad," he called to Van Buren seated at his desk, "just dropped in for a quick word about Karyn."

Van Buren wearily put aside the papers he had been perusing, "What do you want to say about Karyn?"

"Well, I guess you know she's in her eighth month."

"Good God! I've not thought about it, haven't I enough to worry about with your brother lying there unconscious, and your mother daily going more crazy with grief about him? You know damn well she's only got strength enough to leave her bed to visit him." Van Buren shook his head in a distracted way. "Then there's Claudine — do you imagine that I don't know that most of the time she's on drugs — *soft* drugs now, but next it will be heroine or cocaine!" He tore his fingers through his wiry hair, gone almost white since the accident. "What the hell has happened to our family?"

Nicky found it in his heart to pity his father. "Sure Dad, you've more than enough on your plate, so I'll take care of Karyn and the kid . . . I'm going to marry Karyn. I'm going to marry her to give her and the kid a name. I won't lay a hand on her — I'll divorce her immediately. To save her and the kid from disgrace is the only way I can do something for Roy."

Van Buren stared up at his tall son. "Of course you're right. I'm proud of you seeing things so clearly."

"Thanks Father — no one will know about it, except Karyn's family, you and Claudine. It's gotta be absolutely hush-hush or the bloody Press will get hold of the story."

Van Buren nodded. "Yes, yes. Have you made any plans?"

"I was wondering about Las Vegas, it's far enough from New York so the Van Buren name will mean nothing to the locals. There's such a big traffic in marriages, I think we have a chance to get away with it."

"That sounds very sensible, and the divorce?"

"Puerto Rico. A pal at Harvard went to Puerto Rico for a quickie divorce and the story never got out."

"You've planned it all very well."

"Thanks, Dad. Of course I hope to God all this won't be necessary and that Roy comes around in time to marry Karyn. On the level, Dad — what are his chances?" Nicky's deep blue eyes searched Van Buren's brown ones. "Will he ever come out of the coma?"

Van Buren ached to comfort Nicky, but he would not deceive him. "I've told you all I know — these coma cases are unpredictable. He may stay unconscious for God knows how long, but he could suddenly come out so fast it would make your head spin." Drawing hope from his own words, Van Buren added, "So, *if* you have to go through with the marriage, just get yourself back here as fast as you can with the divorce decree in case Roy comes around and wants to marry Karyn himself."

"You bet I will!" Nicky felt hope warming him once more.

"You'd better fly the family 'plane to Las Vegas, gives you more of a chance of escaping the Press."

"Okay Dad — I'll vamoose now — see you later."

The following afternoon Nicky, Karyn, her grandmother and mother sat in the living-room. Nicky had just finished outlining his plans about the marriage to Karyn.

"No, no, I *couldn't* accept your suggestion!" Karyn burst out indignantly. "I don't want your pity, Nicky!"

"For God's sake, honey, it's not pity!" Nicky said. "It's common sense. You *can't* have an illegitimate child! Some society tramps think it's a smart thing to do — but it's not for you. And, Roy's kid must be born a Van Buren."

"I hate the plan — I hate it," Karyn cried hysterically, "I won't do it. No one can make me do it — I belong to Roy . . ."

"We all know that, honey," Nicky said stiffly. "No one is trying to take you from him — we're just trying to help you."

"Karyn your attitude is very selfish," Moira burst out, angrily thinking Karyn must be mad to throw such a lifeline away. "You're thinking only of what *you* want and not what's best for the child, and it's *Roy's* child as well as yours! You've no right to deny his child a name."

"Oh God — I wish you'd all just leave me alone!" Karyn got up and moved lumpishly out of the room.

The others just looked at each other with amazed expressions on their faces.

"Say, I never expected her to act up like that," Nicky said.

"She's terribly overwrought by everything," Joan soothed him, "and who could blame her, but Moira and I can't thank you enough."

"No thanks to me, for God's sake."

"She'll see sense in a little while," Moira said. "I suggest, Nicky, that you go ahead with all the arrangements. If there's no change in Roy she must leave New York in two weeks time. Wouldn't you say so, Mother?"

"Yes, David wants her on the ranch about then, he's not keen on her flying after she's eight and a half months pregnant."

"From Las Vegas, I reckoned I'd fly you up to Doc Murdoch's ranch," Nicky told Joan, "then lam out for Puerto Rico."

"That sounds fine, Nicky," Joan said. "Don't worry about Karyn's little outburst, Moira and I will talk her around to see the wisdom of the plan."

Nicky nodded, but his eyes were clouded

with sadness. "I guess I'll make tracks now."

Both women kissed his cheek, and Moira saw him out.

Some hours later, when Karyn awoke from a sickly sleep, she felt a deep sense of shame at her behaviour. She realised sadly that Nicky's plan was meant to protect her and the baby — she had reacted stupidly and regretted it. She would tell him when he picked her up that evening. She was sitting in the living-room when Joan and Moira came in.

"Feeling okay?" Moira asked Karyn.

"Yes, thanks, and I'm sorry I made such a fuss about Nicky's plan — of course you all are right and I'll do what you say *if* it's necessary."

"Fine," Joan said, relieved that there were to be no more scenes on that score. She sat down, putting the packages she carried beside her, silently grateful at Karyn's change of mood.

"Glad you've seen the light Karyn," Moira said then asked Joan, "What luck, Mother, with an apartment?"

"I looked at three, then decided on a very nice one near the East River — lovely view, close to the Clinic *and* a small Roman Catholic church with a little garden where, on fine days, young Mamas can wheel their babies. I gave a cheque there and then for six months." Then she turned to Karyn, handing her a large package, "Open that, my love." She and Moira watched Karyn as she ripped the paper open and started to pull out baby clothes.

"Oooh . . . how sweet, how sweet," Karyn cooed as she swiftly unpacked half a dozen little woollen jackets, leggings, booties, caps in white, blue, pink. She buried her face in the soft woollies, then looked up. "Oh, Grans, they're lovely! Having these, I know I'm really going to have a baby." Her face broke into a wide smile for the first time since Roy's accident.

"Oh Grans, you're wonderful. I'll just put these lovely little things in my room." Karyn scooped up the baby clothes and, with arms full of them, she left. She wanted to enjoy them alone.

Moira and Joan exchanged tender smiles. "I must change now," Moira said. "Rocky's in town and I'm dining with him. Heavens! I don't know what I would have done without him over the past few months. He's been a tower of strength to me."

Joan warmly kissed Moira's soft cheek. "My poor darling — thank God you had Rocky!"

"You can say that again, Mother — he's

a marvellous man. Well, I'd better make tracks. I'm meeting him at the Plaza."

"Things will be easier for you when Karyn and I have moved to the new apartment, so your friends can pick you up here."

"That's true. I hate going on dates alone, but we've had to conceal the pregnancy."

"Soon life will change, and turn out well for all of us." Joan smiled encouragingly into Moira's doubtful eyes.

"Sure it will, Mother." Moira gave a little laugh thinking of the precarious financial state of her business but, that too, she must not burden her mother with. "Well, I'm off to put on a new face." She planted a kiss on Joan's cheek and dashed to her bedroom.

Twenty-one

The time had arrived when Karyn must leave for Las Vegas. She sat beside Roy's bed and prayed with all of her being for God to allow him to recover. As she leaned over his gaunt face to kiss his forehead, her tears bathed it. "Oh, darling, darling Viking, I've got to go away for a while, but I'm coming back — I'm coming back."

A strong arm went around her shoulders and gently eased her back from the bed. "Time to leave, child," Doctor Van Buren muttered and handed the weeping Karyn over to Claudine, who led her into the corridor.

"Brace up, honey, you're only going for a couple of weeks," Claudine said.

"I know — but I didn't *want* to go at all. You swear you'll call me at the ranch every day to tell me how Roy is?"

"You bet I will, and Carl's in town, thank God. He's gonna take Nicky's place with Roy, so we're gonna keep calling to him. Now, off you go." Claudine kissed Karyn's cheek then whispered in her ear, "Have a boy, just like Roy."

★ ★ ★

The morning was dark, blustery and cold. Joan and Karyn settled back in the black limousine which Moira had booked to drive them to Kennedy Airport.

At the Airport Nicky met them and escorted them to the 'plane. He felt reasonably assured that at this early hour they would not be spotted by any members of the Press, but he was not sanguine about it until they were settled in the eight-seater jet with their seat belts fastened.

"Okay, we're ready to take off," he told them, and disappeared into the cockpit.

Almost immediately they fell asleep and some hours later awoke to brilliant sunshine. Then the 'plane put down and, within minutes they disembarked and Joan's heartbeat quickened as David, smiling widely, came striding toward them. He bent and kissed Joan's cheek, then Karyn's, then he pumped Nicky's hand.

"Good man, you got them here in one piece, shall we lunch in the God awful town?"

"I've got roast beef sandwiches and champagne on board," Nicky said. "We could eat later. I'll just give a few instructions about the 'plane then we can go 'pronto'."

"Right, I've found the place we need — everything's very simple," David told them. They followed him to the hired car and piled in. In silence they drove through dusty streets and turned into a wide thoroughfare flanked by enormous vulgar looking buildings emblazoned, even in sunlight, with brilliant electric signs. Among them David pointed at a small clapboard house painted white and tucked between the huge hotels, "Those are called 'Chapels'," David told them. "They're for quick marriages, the town is full of them."

"It's a disgusting place," Karyn murmured. "I *hate* it!"

"Yeah," Nicky agreed, "we can't quit it soon enough for me."

"Well, this won't take long," David said soothingly, knowing that Karyn and Nicky were both nervous. He stopped the big sedan before a 'Chapel' bearing the sign, 'Kelleys. Instant marriages.'

As David steered them all inside, Karyn was so revolted by the tawdry mockery of marriage she felt hysteria rising in her. It was David's tight grip on her arm that stopped her from running back to the car.

A stocky, red-faced man came up to them, "Hi folks!"

"I called in to see you, Mr Kelly," David

said, "about an hour ago to arrange for a marriage."

"Sure — sure, so this is the happy pair, eh?" He grinned, showing an expanse of oversized false teeth. "Well, well, don't look so glum kids — this won't be painful. You two are the witnesses?" He glanced at Joan and David, who nodded.

"Okay then, here we go." From a nearby table he picked up a worn bible and murmured jocularly to Karyn, "Have trouble in getting the guy here?" He made a face at her pregnant state.

"Get on with the job!" Nicky exploded, bending threateningly over Kelley.

"Okay, okay, Mister." Kelley glanced nervously at Nicky's great height, "You got the names written down for me?" he asked David, who handed him a slip of paper. He glanced at it then rattled off, "Do you, Karyn Kirbo, take Nicholas Van Buren for your husband?"

Karyn managed a nod.

"That's no good, you gotta say, 'I do'," Kelley burst out, and Karyn managed, "I do."

"Okay. And, do you Nicholas Van Buren, take Karyn Kirbo for your wife?"

Nicky swallowed hard, then he said, "I do."

"I now pronounce you man and wife. Gotta ring?" Kelley asked Nicky.

Nicky had bought a plain platinum band but, at that moment, Karyn felt too stricken to lift her hand up until David murmured, "Give Nicky your hand, honey."

She lifted her hand and the sunlight coming through the window shone on Roy's eternity ring on her little finger. Nicky hesitated — feeling like hell, then he made himself slip the wedding ring on.

"That's all there is to it," Kelley was saying. "Just sign the register here." He showed them where and everyone signed. "Right, now let's have the Wasserman certificates with 200 bucks and we'll call it a day."

Joan produced Nicky and Karyn's blood certificates from her bag whilst Nicky flipped $200 from his wallet. Minutes later they were walking to the car, with Joan slipping the marriage licence into her bag.

When they reached the Airport Joan and Karyn went aboard whilst Nicky made arrangements for take off and David turned the hired limousine in. Fifteen minutes later they were winging towards San Francisco.

Throughout the short flight Karyn did not talk, her thoughts were with Roy. She longed to be able to telephone Claudine for news of him. She would be in purgatory until

Nicky was in Puerto Rico and the divorce was established. Exhausted with sorrow, fears, hopes, speculations, she fell asleep.

Seated behind her, Joan and David sat hand in hand. Joan murmured, "Thank God for this morning's work, and thank you too, darling, for everything you've done to help. Honestly darling, we'd have been lost without your constant support. I'll for ever be grateful to you. But tell me is something wrong? I seem to feel that you're depressed —" her eyes raked his, "I hope I'm wrong."

"Your extra-sensory perception was always good. Yes, I am depressed, but I didn't want to burden you with it until Karyn was out of the woods."

"No, no, I've poured all my troubles on to you, so now share yours with me — tell me, what is it?"

"Well, it's Margaret. Some months ago I asked her for a divorce, quite believing she would easily agree, but she said she'd think about it. Then, two days ago, when I brought up the subject again, she told me that she needed a husband to escort her about socially, that's all she wanted from me, but she'd never free me."

"Oh, David . . ." For all the months of helping Karyn through her grief Joan had enshrined in her heart the thought that someday she and David would marry — it had been her support — now everything was shattered. "How cruel of her, when she doesn't want you — I mean, not as a husband — she has no affection even for you."

"Cruel of her by God! And, since you've come back into my life everything has changed for me. I have someone to live for, a reason to exist apart from my medicine. But now how the hell can I ask you to come and live at the ranch when I've no hope of marrying you eventually?"

"Don't think on the negative side, darling, there must be ways of making Margaret give you a divorce."

"You bet I don't intend to take her refusal lying down!"

"David, we'll work something out, we won't let this selfish woman ruin the good years we can have together. Let's discuss it all again, after Karyn's delivery."

"By God! It's wonderful of you to take it so well."

He caught her chin in strong fingers, tilted her face up to his and kissed her.

After Nicky had brought the 'plane down in San Francisco, they all said speedy good-byes for he had to take off at once for New

York to catch the evening 'plane for Puerto Rico.

Later when Joan, Karyn and David reached Aurora Ranch, David insisted Karyn go straight to bed and Joan went immediately to telephone New York to tell Moira the marriage had gone according to plan.

"Oh God, I'm so relieved!" Moira cried. "All day I've been terrified that some damn thing would crop up to put a spanner in the wheels, but now it's really done."

"Yes, so you can stop worrying so much and take a little care of *yourself* darling, you're working so hard and, with all this trouble on top of it, I'm anxious about you."

"No need to be, Mother darling, and at least my personal luck is looking up. Rocky 'phoned from Washington — he's at a legal convention there — and, out of a clear blue sky, his wife wants a divorce! She's fallen in love with a guy ten years younger than herself."

If only such good fortune would come to David, Joan thought, as she said, "But that sounds very hopeful for you and Rocky."

"Maybe it won't make any difference to him. I've told you he's never dangled wedding bells before me. Still, we'll see. He gets in tomorrow."

"Well, 'phone me, darling, if you have good news."

"You bet, Mother — well, nite now."

"Good night my pet, God bless you."

Moira was rearranging the golden tulips Rocky had sent when the buzzer rang and she went rather nervously to answer it. "Hello, hello," she said lightly, as Rocky came inside.

He leaned down to kiss her, then handed her a long beribboned package. "For you, honey."

"What on earth's in it? It's quite heavy."

"Yeah," he grinned. "I reckon it should have some weight." He eased his big shoulders out of his overcoat and left it on a chair, then followed Moira into the living-room.

"A present for me, and it's not even my birthday," Moira cooed. "Will you mix yourself a drink, Rocky, I can't wait to open this."

"Go ahead."

She tore the paper open then lifted the lid off a shiny maroon box, and gasped, "Not mink! But every woman's dream — SABLE!" Gently, she pulled the coat free of layers of tissue papers.

"Oh, Rocky — it's divine!" She laid her cheek against the soft silky fur, then she slipped the full length coat on, staring up at him with eyes round in delighted wonder.

"Sure glad you like it, honey."

"But . . . but . . . honestly, I can't accept a gift like this — it's too valuable!" She knew it would have strings attached and she had no intention of becoming Rocky's mistress. She had fought him off for months, now a $20,000 sable coat could not buy her, the only currency she would accept was marriage.

"*Why* can't you accept it?" He chuckled, amused that for once she was at a loss for a reply, usually she was so quick-witted.

"Well . . . I just can't . . ." She started slipping the coat off. "Surely you can understand? I mean . . ."

"You reckon there are strings attached?"

She gave a little nod, "We've gone over all of that many times, haven't we? And you know I don't have affairs."

"Yeah, it's one of the thousand and one reasons I got stuck on you. Okay honey, you're right, there are strings attached to the coat, but they're tied to a marriage licence. I'll soon be free."

Her heart flew to her throat. "You mean that . . ."

"Yeah, yeah, do you dig the idea?"

"*Do* I? — Oh Rocky!" She flung herself

into his outstretched arms and he crushed her in a bear hug. "I've been trying for months not to fall in love with you Rocky, darling."

"And, for months I've been trying to think up ways of getting a divorce to marry you — now Christ! Everything is solved and soon I'll be free. I'll be the God darned proudest son-of-a-bitch in the whole country to have you, a real lady, for a wife."

"What a lovely thing to say, Rocky, and I'll be the proudest woman to have a husband like you."

"Won't be long before we can tie the knot. The divorce will be a quickie in Mexico — then pronto, it's us in about three weeks from now. Oh, I almost forgot — I've something else for you." He let go of her and, digging into his pocket, pulled out a small green velvet box which he thrust into her hand.

Trembling with excitement and joy at the sudden wonderful turn in her life, she touched the little spring, the lid flew up and she gazed, almost unbelievingly, at a huge blue-white marquee cut diamond.

"Rocky — it's a treasure!" She whispered almost reverently, gazing up at the man whose face might have been carved from rock granite. "It's a *dream* ring!" and she murmured "Ooh — it's magnificent!"

She looked up at Rocky with the delight of a child.

"Honey — honey, I'm wild about you," he said. "You've got such class, such style. Your English voice, your manners, I go for all of you in one helluva big way."

How good it was to be loved again. "Rocky dearest, darling Rocky, I am so happy." Her long eyelashes were wet with tears. "Silly me — I'm crying — heavens!"

Some hours later when he had gone she dialled Aurora Ranch. She could not wait another second to fill her mother's heart with joy at her marvellous news.

Twenty-two

Claudine lay on her bed smoking. She was well aware that she was leaning too heavily on grass but, without it she would be unable to endure the hours sitting beside Roy.

Then she remembered that she must make her daily 'phone call to Karyn. She half sat up, reached for the telephone, switched it on to an outside line then dialled Aurora Ranch. After a minute's wait Karyn answered.

"Hi, Karyn — how're ya?"

"Oh, okay — I've been waiting for your call, how's Roy?"

"He's no worse so that's something."

"Yeah. Oh, I wish the baby would come soon."

"Don't we all! Well, I expect Nicky should be back from Puerto Rico in a couple of days. Boy how I miss him. Well mind how you go, honey."

"Sure, and you too, Claudine, I'll soon be back to help with Roy."

"Okay, call ya tomorrow." Claudine replaced the telephone on its cradle.

Karyn hung up and went slowly out to the

porch where David sat in a reclining chair smoking his pipe, and Joan sat knitting a baby jacket.

"No bad news?" David asked, seeing Karyn's glum expression.

"Nope. Roy's just the same, but I'm also worried about Claudine. She sounded stoned again. Of course she's having an extra tough time without Nicky and me, even though Carl's with her." Karyn shuddered at the mental picture of Roy with Claudine seated by his bed. She moved slowly and lumpishly about the porch. "Oh, I wish this birth business would happen!"

"How are you feeling, honey?"

"Awful, D.D.! Restless, uncomfortable, frantic."

David got to his feet. "I'll 'phone the nurse, I think it's time she got out here."

"You think the baby might come today?" Joan asked anxiously."

"Could be, it looks pretty low." He went into the house.

"Darling, you've no labour pains yet?" Joan asked.

"No Grans, I wish I had! I'm so fed-up with the waiting — waiting — waiting!"

Just before lunch Miss Humphries, a pink faced, middle-aged nurse arrived and, after introductions, they all went in to lunch.

They were finishing the first course when a splitting pain tore through Karyn and she screamed.

"That was damned nasty D.D. Will the baby come soon?"

"Probably, now go with nurse Humphries and she'll get you ready."

When they had gone Joan said, "I'm mad, David, but I feel so apprehensive."

"Don't worry, I'm anticipating an easy birth."

"Thank God for that, please don't let her have too much pain! You *will* give her something to help her, won't you darling?"

"Of course I will, but first the pains must be coming every minute so she can do some pushing, but I won't let her suffer."

An hour later Karyn's pains were coming every two minutes and Joan pleaded with her.

"Don't *contract*, darling! Bear *down*, hang onto a piece of furniture and bear *down, down!*"

"Oh Grans!" Karyn half screamed, "It's awful — awful!"

"I know it, my darling, I'm so sorry, I'll get D.D." Joan rushed into the living-room where David sat talking quietly to Nurse Humphries. "Her pains are very severe! *Do* help her!"

"Right, we will. Okay, Nurse Humphries, take her into our protem delivery room and you Joan go for a walk in the garden."

It seemed to Joan that she had been pacing up and down for an eternity when at last David came out.

"All's well! A splendid seven pound boy!"

"Thank God!" she cried and rushed up the steps to throw herself into his arms.

He hugged her. "It was an easy birth with very little pain. She's sleeping now, but come and see a future President."

Joan stared down at the tiny marvel of humanity, his head capped with golden fuzz. The sight of him made her feel weak with emotions — poor baby — with his father so afflicted. Joan glanced at Karyn, her beautiful face was now peaceful in sleep.

Then Joan went straight to telephone the wonderful news to a joyful Moira. Joan's second telephone call was to Claudine at the Clinic.

"Karyn's had a boy, he's perfect, with golden hair, of course she's going to call him Christian — the name Roy chose."

"Oh God! A boy! That's great!" Claudine called down the telephone, "Give her my love — now I'll go and tell my father."

Leaving the booth on the corridor,

200

Claudine dashed to her father's private suite and rushed in.

"Is there a change in Roy?" He jumped up eagerly.

She shook her head. "No, no, I came to tell you, you've a grandson, born a couple of hours ago. A perfect child with golden hair like Roy's."

He winced as if with pain, then muttered, "Roy has a son! Oh Christ — he should have been there!"

"*You* should have been there!" Claudine spat the words out bitterly. "He's *your* grandson, so *your* responsibility whilst Roy is unconscious. Nicky's done his share by giving your grandson a legitimate name, but you've bloody well done nothing! I don't care about Mother — she's crazy, but you — you! I *hate* you for the way you've neglected Karyn."

She rushed away, slamming the door then, seated by Roy's bedside she gathered her calm. How dared she say those awful things to her father? But the truth had burst from her heart.

In the shadowy room, lit by a lamp at the back of Roy's head, Claudine stared down at his wasted body. His eyes were closed, his mouth was shut, she knew he was in a sleeping cycle. Claudine bent low over him, her face almost touching his.

"Roy — Roy, you have a *son!* Oh, my beloved brother, I hope that somehow you can hear me. You have a son, with hair like yours!"

He lay motionless — God! Would he *always* be like this? Her eyes fixed on the plastic tube stuck in the hole in his throat. If she were to pull it out of the hole in his throat he would stop breathing! He would die! But wasn't he already dead? Would he have wished to lie here all these months like a zombie? Never! *Not Roy!* He would have opted for real death.

Should she do it for him? She shuddered with the enormity of her thoughts — to end Roy's half-life! But he would want her to. Her hand stretched out stiffly to seize the mouth of the tube, to jerk it out of the hole in the throat — her fingers hovered over it — but they would not move, they seemed paralysed. *She could not do it!* She could not! Tomorrow might be miracle day, tomorrow he might recover! Christ knew, the miracle was long overdue — but she must wait.

As soon as she reached home she went to her room to telephone Nicky at his hotel in Puerto Rico. When he answered the telephone, the thickness of his voice told her he was drunk.

"Nicky — hi — we have a *nephew* — how about that?" A pause on the other end, then Nicky's subdued voice. "Christ! Is that right?"

"Yeah, I thought you'd want to know."

"You're damned right."

"And Karyn's okay."

"That's great! How about Roy?"

"The same. You okay? You sound sloshed."

"I am, been sloshed since I arrived. Got a new Spanish friend — a great girl, Carlotta."

Poor Nicky, Claudine understood that he was trying, for a little while, to forget the tragedy of Roy. "Glad that you've found a friend, Nicky, but when are you coming back?"

"Tomorrow — divorce all sewn up. A nephew eh? Great! See you, Claudine — mind how you go."

"You too — watch your step. Have Carlotta stand by until you're airbound."

"Will do."

They both hung up.

Twenty-three

"He's the most beautiful baby! Absolutely perfect!" Moira cooed delightedly down at Christian, whom she cuddled in her arms. She, Joan and Karyn, had just returned from Kennedy Airport to the apartment on the East River.

"His eyes are just like Roy's," Karyn said proudly, "and look at his hair! It could have been cut off Roy's head and stuck on to Christian's. Now I must take him, it's his feeding time. Isn't it wonderful that I've got so much milk?"

"It's splendid, breast-feeding is the best thing for him."

Moira led the way into the bedroom allotted to Christian and the nurse, due to arrive soon. Karyn settled onto a chair, unzipped the top of her dress and gave Christian the breast.

"I'll go and see to the luggage, honey," Moira told her daughter.

As she opened the front door to admit the doorman with the bags, she was surprised to see Claudine with him.

"Ah, Mrs Kirbo," Claudine said apologetically, "I hope it's okay, but I couldn't wait to see Karyn and my nephew. I'd have been at the 'plane, but I stayed with Roy."

"Come in, honey, of course. Karyn's feeding Christian but I'll tell her you're here."

"Claudine!" Karyn's excited call came from the bedroom. "Come in — come in!"

Claudine rushed to the room then, at the open doorway, stopped at the sight of Karyn cuddling Christian to her breast. He was making a little cosy, sucking sound.

"Claudine, come and look at our boy!"

Claudine approached slowly, her eyes clamped to Christian's little face. "Ooh . . . ooh, he's cute! He's absolutely gorgeous, and so like Roy."

"The living image, isn't he? But, tell me about Roy."

"The same, always the same." Claudine was suddenly gripped by such fierce rebellion over Roy's cruel condition, she felt she must throw up.

Moira steered her to the bathroom and held her head over the toilet bowl.

When they returned to the bedroom, Karyn had finished the feeding, and Christian now lay asleep in his crib, looking like a china doll.

"I'm going to the Clinic now," Karyn quietly announced.

"Don't go today, darling; you should rest after the journey," Moira said.

"I *must* go to Roy! How do we *really* know if he hears what we say or not? Just because he doesn't react to our voices doesn't mean he doesn't hear us. I *must* go! I want to tell him about Christian — oh God, I wish I could take Christian to show him to Roy."

"Nicky and Carl are downstairs," Claudine said. "They didn't like to come up when you'd just arrived, but may I get them? They're just wild to see Christian."

"Oh yes, yes, bring them up." Karyn longed to show them her baby.

When Claudine rushed away, Karyn swiftly changed into what had been a favourite dress of Roy's. Maybe this very day he would come out of his terrible sleep.

Then Nicky and Carl came diffidently into the apartment.

The young men, feeling strangely stirred, stood looking down at the baby, then Nicky gasped, "By God! He doesn't look real, he's so perfect." His voice shook with suppressed emotion — Roy's kid — oh Christ! and he can't even see him!

"He's really sumpin' special." There was a reverent look in Carl's dark eyes.

Karyn felt such happiness in her baby, she imparted it to the others so that suddenly they began to feel optimistic again about Roy's recovery. A few minutes later, they left to visit him.

Days slipped into weeks but there was no change in Roy. Karyn was utterly obsessed by his condition, she lived in a cocoon of Roy's tragedy, outside events could hardly force their way into her consciousness. She managed to be polite about her mother's marriage in Reno; she was glad she was so happy, and she liked Rocky with his strong Texan face. He obviously adored her mother, but Karyn was not a part of their happiness and had no interest in their plans to find a mansion in Washington, where they now spent most of their time.

Winter succumbed to spring's enchantment, but Karyn observing her duty to daily wheel Christian's perambulator in the nearby little park, had no room in her being to glory in earth's awakening. She was unaware of the tender new greenery, or the pale hued blossoms. One thought possessed her — Roy *must* recover!

In her spacious, luxurious bedroom, Ann Van Buren paced the Aubusson rug in agitation. Suddenly she stopped and, white-faced, confronted Nicky and Claudine.

"Your father's only just told me Nicky that

you married that — that — tramp, and she's given birth to a boy."

"You know that Karyn's no tramp!"

"Be silent!" Ann ordered. "You, Nicky, — my beloved son, how could you deceive me like that!"

"I didn't deceive you, Mother. I just didn't tell you that I was marrying Karyn because I wanted to avoid a scene."

"God help me, what have I done to deserve such treatment from you, Nicky?" Ann's great eyes glared at him. "And, how cruel not to tell me of my grandson's birth. He's three months old and I, his paternal grandmother, have never even seen him! Still, Nicky, how clever of you to have got an *immediate* divorce so that girl could not trap you."

"Oh Christ, Mother, how wrong you are! The reason I got an immediate divorce was because that's the only way Karyn would marry — she wanted to be free for Roy, if he recovered. You don't know what a wonderful person she is."

"Protect *her* against *me!* How can you, Nicky — I, your Mother, who adores you."

"Oh Mother, I'm trying to make you realize how wrong you are about Karyn. It's for your own sake — so that you don't keep on cutting off your nose to spite your face."

"And exactly what do you mean by that?"

"It's obvious! If you keep on hating Karyn, you'll never have a chance to see Christian."

She gave a shrill laugh. "Clever as you think you are, with your one year of law at Harvard, you've evidently not heard that a father has rights over his child! You will *order* this woman to bring my grandson to see me!"

"For God's sake, Mother," Claudine jumped disgustedly to her feet, "how can Nicky give orders to Karyn about her child?"

"Because the child has been registered as Nicky's son, so he can exert paternal rights."

"I haven't got *any* legal rights over Christian — naturally, I gave Karyn full custody of her own child in the divorce suit."

Ann took a backward step and stood swaying. "Oh no! No! You couldn't have been such a fool! You let a Van Buren boy slip away from the family! Oh — I'm ill, Nicky, help me to lie down."

Loathing the whole messy business, Nicky went to Ann, who immediately collapsed against him. He caught her in his arms, carried her to the bed and settled her on it.

"She'll be okay, Nicky." Claudine was utterly weary of her mother's play-acting, but she followed through with the farce and placed a damp cloth on her forehead. Soon

Ann's eyelids fluttered open and she looked appealingly up at Nicky.

"My darling, you must go at once to your Father's lawyer! File a suit for joint custody for Christian — we will fight Karyn for him. *I* must have the boy! He belongs to me, and your young sisters, they also have the right to their nephew!"

"Yeah, yeah," Nicky nodded, "now you rest and we'll discuss everything later." He glanced at his wristwatch. "We've got to make tracks, we're meeting Carl at the Clinic — we're into a new experiment. We all talk to Roy as if he were part of our general chat. Maybe our combined voices will get through to him."

Talk of Roy's tragedy swept everything else from Ann's mind. "Yes, go — go! Try everything on earth to save him."

"Sure, sure — now you rest!" Nicky bent and perfunctorily touched his lips to her forehead, then he and Claudine left.

Outside, they walked down a corridor of the huge house. "My God, Nicky, she's *really* crazy!" Claudine said. "Do you think she'll go through with a law-suit to try to get joint custody of Christian?"

"Jesus! She's mad enough for anything, and she's the same woman who offered $150,000 for Karyn to have an abortion.

Now, she *wants* the child! I'll see everyone in hell before I'd upset my divorce decree and claim half-custody of Christian, but I guess we gotta warn Karyn about this."

Twenty-four

That weekend when David arrived in New York he went straight to Joan and Karyn's apartment, and was glad to find Joan alone.

"Lovely that you're here, darling. Karyn's at the Clinic."

They sat together on the sofa, "You look tired, Joan darling, are you feeling okay?"

"Fine, but a new worry has sprung up." She told him about Ann Van Buren's determination to have joint custody of Christian.

"It's what I foresaw, perhaps I'd better go and talk to Peter Van Buren about it."

"That might help. Of course I 'phoned Moira immediately — she's in Washington with Rocky and when she told Rocky about it he said that Ann Van Buren will have very little chance of winning a half custody suit."

"Good — but I think I should try and cut the whole business off at the roots. Van Buren has got to control his mad wife. Now, can you come out to dinner with me tonight — you're surely not still nervous of leaving Karyn alone?"

"Of course, I'd love to come. In any case, Claudine, Nicky and Carl are coming to supper with her. It's fallen into a habit and I'm glad, it seems to be a help to all of them to be together. Now, I'll go and make some tea."

"Fine, and I'll ring Van Buren to make an appointment to go over after tea."

In Van Buren's office, David sat in a leather armchair, shocked by the way sorrow had scored Peter's face.

"I know you've more than your load of trouble, Peter, but I'm afraid I must speak of this business of Ann trying to get joint custody of Roy's child. It's preposterous!"

"Is it?" Van Buren muttered, "The boy is *my* grandson and I believe grandparents have some rights in connection with their grandchildren."

David was so astonished that it took several seconds before he could talk. "Good God — this is a surprise! You mean you'll back Ann's claim if she goes to Law?"

"It will be *my* claim too." Peter spoke grimly. "Do you think I'd let Roy's son remain with that girl and her family without enjoying the benefits of being raised as a Van Buren? Never!"

"But she'll fight your claim — think of the scandal. The media will go wild with such a story, can't you see it? While Roy's half dead, his brother marries and fathers Karyn's child."

"You don't have to tell me the consequences of our law-suit but, between two evils I'll choose the minor one. The most important thing is the Van Buren boy's future." He shrugged with an infinite weariness, "But we'll do nothing yet — by some miracle Roy might still come around and that would change everything."

"Well, well, I didn't think you'd be so interested in Christian, but I must tell you that Karyn and her family will fight you up to the Supreme Court — Karyn's mother has married one of the finest lawyers in the country and he swears you haven't a chance of winning."

"Perhaps not, but if that's the case, I wouldn't put it past Ann to kidnap Christian." His dark eyes stared compellingly into David's angry blue eyes. "She can sign her name to a huge sum of money — enough to pay a skilful baby-snatcher."

"But, Peter, that sounds like a threat!"

"No, I'm just pointing out a possibility." Van Buren spoke in cold, measured tones.

Inwardly furious, David stood up, "I'll be on my way now."

"If you want to help Karyn, make her realise that we have parental rights, in place

214

of Roy, over Roy's son. She can spare herself a lot of grief if she listens to reason."

"And that means handing Christian over for part of his life, to you?" David's voice was thick with irony.

Van Buren nodded, "That would be just, the boy *is* a Van Buren." He spoke with an almost savage pride.

Years of discipline helped David control his anger; he knew nothing would be gained by quarrelling with Van Buren; later, perhaps he might talk sense into him.

"Tell me, Peter, as one medical man to another, what actually *are* Roy's chances of recovery?"

Van Buren shut his eyes as if to close out pain, then he opened them and muttered hoarsely, "The world's finest neurologists have all said, 'Impossible to see a chance of recovery'. For months, my love has insisted upon keeping him alive on the respiratory machine." He flung his arms wide in a gesture of appeal, "But, am I right to do so when I know the truth? But, Christ, I haven't the courage to cut off my beloved son's life."

David's anger dissipated for he could not help pitying Peter. He spoke softly. "It takes gut-courage to stop the respirators, even though you know Roy's case is hopeless."

Peter turned his haggard face to look

squarely into David's face. "Would you have the gut-courage to do it if you were in my place?"

"I'm not sure I would — but you've got to think of Claudine and Karyn, their lives are almost lived beside Roy's bed. Can you imagine what traumas are building up inside them? Constantly suffering for Roy, and Nicky and Carl too who've given up Harvard to be with Roy. And it must be a constant hell for Ann to see him deteriorating. Better for all of them if it ended."

Van Buren nodded heavily. "Yeah, yeah, I must make myself accept the truth that my brilliant son actually died months ago."

"Then, in the name of God, let his poor body go! Why keep him alive like a vegetable? Doctors are often faced with this dilemma, they've got to have the courage to do what's right!"

"Yeah, yeah, but to stop the machines, — I couldn't . . ."

"Sometimes there comes a time when ruthlessness must override love and sentiment. Leave the job to a trusted assistant." David waited a moment then added softly, "I'll bet Roy would have wanted that tube pulled out."

Back at the apartment, David felt he must

account truthfully to Joan all that had passed between Van Buren and himself.

Terribly perturbed, Joan murmured, "It's too awful to have this added worry hanging over us, but as long as Roy stays alive there'll be no law suit."

"That's it. Meanwhile, perhaps things might ease up a bit if Karyn would let Ann Van Buren see Christian, after all she *is* his grandmother."

"Well, you may be right. I'll talk to Karyn about it."

When Karyn came in Joan told her, "D.D. and I were thinking that, perhaps, you should let Mrs Van Buren see Christian."

Karyn winced as if with pain, "No, no, I'll *never* let her see him!"

"Darling, she *is* his grandmother, surely she has a right to just *see* him?"

"She hasn't! She hasn't!" Karyn half screamed. "She didn't want him to be born! She's wicked! I won't have her near Christian — her evil thoughts might harm him."

"Karyn honey," David saw she was near hysteria, "forget about it now. How about opening up a bottle of your Gran's pink champagne."

"Good idea." Joan gladly agreed, smiling at David, "But terribly extravagant of you to have sent a whole case."

In the well patronized restaurant 'Chianti', on New York's East side at a corner table Nicky, Carl and Claudine sat drinking cognac.

"So, how much longer are we going to let the hell drag on?" Claudine spoke in a quietly challenging voice. "Why are we so chicken?"

"Nobody's chicken for Christ's sake!" Nicky muttered angrily. "It's just that the act will be *irrevocable.*" His blue eyes blazed at Claudine, "You get it? No bloody use regretting it once we've done it."

"Sure, sure, we've all thought of that, man," Carl's face was drawn with grief, "but Claudine's damn right. We're acting like weak-livered punks. Can you imagine how sore Roy would be with us for letting him lie there like that for a year?"

"I'll tell you something for sure," Claudine stared solemnly at both of them, "It's driving Karyn bats. I mean it — bats! She's so God damn sure that Roy understands all her babbling about Christian that, one day, she'll crack."

"I think Claudine's right," Carl said. "We've gotta save Karyn from any more of this Hell, or the next thing you know, she'll be in a loony bin and Christian won't have a father *or* mother."

"Just what my mother would like," Nicky muttered savagely. "She could grab the kid."

"Over my dead body." Claudine spoke between clenched teeth. "I swear I'd bolt with him — to Europe or somewhere, but I'd never let Mother get her claws on him. Carl tell Nicky what your uncle in Boston said."

Carl lifted his eyes from his brandy to look deeply into Nicky's eyes, hoping to calm his doubts. "My uncle Joseph is a Jesuit priest and, yesterday, I 'phoned him and asked him what view the Catholic Church takes about cases where the brain is dead, but the body lives through a respirator. Is it a sin to deny the person artificial means of prolonging life?"

"Yeah, yeah," Nicky snapped irritably, "so what was the answer?"

"He said — everything should be done to keep someone alive except in extraordinary circumstances, when the burden becomes impossible to support — then," he paused for a second, and slowly said, "then a human being is permitted to die. He said respirators represent 'extraordinary' means of keeping a near-dead person alive — and, Nicky, the Catholic Church says there's no *moral* need to do so."

"So it's not murder," Nicky whispered, his face twisting with pain, "to pull the respirator out?"

"No, no, no!" Carl assured him, "And, if you two wish it, I'll do it alone."

"Oh no, man." Nicky shook his head, "We'll do it the way we planned. We'll all hold the plastic tube in the hole in his throat, and pull it together. Then we'll call a nurse and say we found him like that."

Twenty-five

At ten A.M. Nicky, Claudine and Carl arrived at the Clinic. They had deliberately got high on marijuana to help them to go through with their plans.

Leaving the elevator they nodded toward a nurse and started for Roy's room, but the nurse called out.

"I'm sorry . . . I'm afraid you can't go into Mr Roy Van Buren's room."

"Just *why* not?" Nicky exploded furiously, wondering if some bastard had guessed at their plan?

"Those are Doctor Van Buren's orders, sir." The nurse lost none of her calm as she faced the three agitated looking young people.

"But *why* has my father given such an order?" Claudine demanded. "We've been coming in every morning for months."

"Well, Miss Van Buren," the nurse hesitated, then went on, "I'm sorry to tell you, your brother died during the night."

"Died!" Claudine screamed, then broke into hysterical laughter as Carl muttered, "Died?" While Nicky demanded in a choked voice, *"How did he die? How"* Sweet Jesus! They had been spared the unspeakable job, from committing the unspeakable act. "What *caused* his death?"

"But, Mr Van Buren, you surely know he's been in a dying condition for months?" The nurse spoke gently, "Though of course, it's always a blow when death actually comes. Your father left word that he wants to see all of you in his office."

"Yeah . . . yeah, we'll go see him . . . Did my brother suffer?" Nicky muttered.

"Not at all; he slipped peacefully away."

"Sure, sure — come on, let's go." Nicky led the way down a side hall. "Claudine, for Christ's sake stop squalling, you know it's what we wanted."

"Yeah, yeah, and I'm so grateful it — happened naturally — that we — that we . . ."

"Yeah, honey, I feel the same." Carl's arm around her shoulders gave her a reassuring squeeze.

When they walked into Peter Van Buren's office they were shocked by his haggard face, and Nicky burst out, "Dad, don't let it throw you. We really lost Roy months ago." He sank into a chair. "Best thing that it's over at last."

Van Buren's burning eyes scrutinized Claudine's face, then Carl's solemn countenance. "You two feel like Nicky does?"

"Sure we do, Dad," sobbed Claudine. "You did everything on God's earth to save him. You must never forget that." Suddenly a terrible truth flashed to Claudine — her father had disconnected Roy from the respirator! Longing to help free him from feelings of guilt, she burst out, "It's happened for the best, we all know that. I only hope Karyn sees it that way."

"And your mother too."

"We'd better go tell Karyn." Nicky stood up. "We don't want her turning up here to be told about it. We'll come back if you like, Father."

"No, meet me at home about twelve or so — I'll need moral support when I tell your mother."

As they left his office, Van Buren dropped his face in his hands. Thank God they had suspected nothing.

Joan was in the living-room dancing a gurgling Christian on her knee and Karyn was in the bedroom dressing for her usual visit to Roy, when Nicky, Claudine and Carl arrived. Joan immediately saw Claudine's red-rimmed eyes, but before she could ask if she had been crying, Christian started to bounce himself up and down, arms held up to Nicky.

"Look, he wants to go to you, Nicky," Joan smiled widely, "like he did yesterday. He's really mad about you."

So choked up he could not trust himself to speak, Nicky's big hands took Christian. The soft warmth of the little body, so over-powered Nicky he had a terror he would weep. Silently, he carried Christian to the end of the room pretending to look out of the window on the East River.

"What's happened?" Joan anxiously asked the grim-faced Carl, and red-eyed Claudine.

Claudine mouthed the words, "Roy . . . he's gone."

"Oh!" Joan gasped, her body going weak with distress, but then relief came sweeping through her. The long Gethsemane for those who loved him had ended at last. "My dears, I'm so sorry," she murmured.

At that moment Karyn came in and seeing Christian in Nicky's arms she smiled, think-ing, that's how Roy will look holding his son — the two blond heads together. The next second she saw Claudine's distressed face and Carl's tightly compressed lips.

"What's happened? What's happened?"

"It's Roy . . ." Carl muttered. "It's over."

"That's a *lie* Carl!" Karyn threw the words at him. "A lie, because everyone's trying to stop me going to him! But it won't work!"

Her voice rose hysterically. "*Nothing* will stop me going to him, I tell you!" Her big eyes blazed with defiance. "Yesterday he was much better . . . I . . . I . . . Oh no! Now . . . he's . . ." her voice trailed away as she stared at Claudine's contracted face. "It's true, Claudine?" came Karyn's hoarse whisper, appealing for a denial, but Claudine gave an abrupt nod.

"Sit down, my darling." Joan led Karyn to a chair.

No one spoke in the room, everyone was silenced by grief, bound together in their pain. Then some pigeons settled on the window sill and Christian squealed with delight.

It had the effect of a clap of thunder; everyone suddenly moved, the baby's joyous cries had broken death's hold on them.

"He loves watching the pigeons," Joan said gently, "and what a fancy he's taken to Nicky. It's quite remarkable." That will help Nicky she thought, then left Karyn's side to go to Claudine. "Would you like some coffee, my dear?"

"No thank you, I'd like a brandy, please. I guess Carl and Nicky would too."

"Shall I pour them, Mrs Clements?" Carl stood up.

"Please do." Joan nodded toward the

cocktail cabinet. "Karyn darling, will you have a brandy?"

Karyn did not answer, she just stared straight ahead seeing nothing, there was nothing to see, there was nothing anywhere. Nothing left in the world for her but to care for Christian whom Roy had never even seen.

"I think I'll make some coffee anyhow," Joan said, leaving for the kitchen.

Turning around from the window, holding the gurgling Christian, Nicky saw Karyn with the half-mad expression on her face, "You okay, honey?" he asked.

She gave no reply, just stared ahead with unseeing, unblinking eyes, until Claudine said, "Snap out of it, Karyn! You're not the only one suffering over Roy, we all are. Nicky and I have always had him in our lives, there was never a time when he wasn't there, and Carl's been his best buddy since they were in play school — we're all feeling like bloody hell."

"Yes — yes," Karyn slowly murmured, "he was your brother and Carl's friend — but for me? . . . He was . . . he was . . . all . . . all . . . oh God!"

Bursting into tears she dashed away to her bedroom where she threw herself face down on the bed. Even from the living-room they could hear her shattering sobs.

"Thank God we have Christian — he's not only Karyn's — he belongs to all of us." Nicky pressed his face against the baby's soft little body and, squealing with delight, Christian's chubby hands grabbed his uncle's thick golden hair.

Joan came in with coffee. "I've made plenty so . . ." She broke off hearing Karyn's convulsive sobbing. "Please, Carl," she pushed the tray at him and rushed to the bedroom, closing the door behind her. She went to sit on the edge of the bed, and cradled Karyn's shaking shoulders in her arms.

"Oh, my poor, poor darling, I know what you're suffering but, try to remember that if it was God's will for Roy never to recover, it's best that he's gone. God wanted him, darling, that's why He took him. This is a terrible sorrow for you to bear, but God will give you strength. Let's say an 'Our Father', out loud for the repose of Roy's soul."

When the prayer was finished Karyn's racking sobs grew less, then as Joan went on gently consoling her they gradually died.

"I don't want to be a coward, Grans," Karyn murmured, "and Claudine is right, I am not the only one suffering — they are too."

"Yes, and you must help them, you must be strong so that they can lean on you a little. You've been blessed by such a lovely little son, so a part of Roy will always be with you."

There was a knock on the door. "Come in," Joan called, and Claudine came in, cuddling Christian in her arms.

"He's growing sleepy, Karyn, I thought I should settle him in his crib before we go. We promised Dad we'd be home when he breaks the news to Mother." She kissed Christian's fat little legs and laid him in the crib. "Thank God we've got him." With a wave to Karyn, she said, "We'll come by later, honey."

Joan saw Claudine and the boys out, then leaned her shoulders and head wearily back against the locked door. Thank God Karyn's macabre death-watch was over at last. She would suffer of course, for her love for Roy had been obsessive, but with time life would resume normality for her.

Then, a terrifying thought stabbed through her mind. Great God! Now that Roy was dead, would the Van Burens institute legal proceedings to gain part-time custody of Christian? She must telephone Moira at once about Roy's death then, when she arrived, discuss this new threat with her.

Thank heaven it was Friday so David would be arriving from California. She desperately needed him to lean upon.

Roy was quietly buried in the family plot in the Newport cemetery. The Press gave the event very little coverage, for there was nothing sensational in it. The Van Burens did not invite Karyn to attend the funeral, nor would she have gone had they done so.

"It's not Roy they're burying," she wept in her mother's arms, "it's just his poor body. Roy's spirit is *here* with me."

Karyn told no one that she saw Roy everywhere, that he was always with her, not the poor, unconscious Roy, but her magnificent Viking with his athletic body filled with strength, his Pacific-Ocean blue eyes laughing, his teeth glistening, his strong hands reaching out to hold her.

This constant vision of Viking, which was so clear to her, helped to sustain her as the next aching month plodded by, but she ate little, slept little, could hardly bother to pull her jeans and T-shirt on, to comb her hair. She made every excuse not to go out, even to wheel Christian's pram. She lost weight, and her face wore a disturbing pallor. She only came to life a little when Claudine, Nicky and Carl came each day. The four of them spent hours together gaining comfort from one another's presence.

Moira again arrived from Washington. This time she was determined to take Karyn and Christian back with her, but Karyn demurred.

"I'd like to come with you, Mother, and I know you're right that Grans badly needs a rest, but let me stay here a little longer, I want to be around Claudine, Nicky and Carl."

"Yes, I can understand that, but honey, a change would be good for you and we've also got to think of Grans. Poor darling, she must be allowed to have a little life of her own."

"Don't let's worry about that," Joan forced a light tone, as she arranged the long-stemmed red roses Moira had brought. "You know how marvellously patient D.D. is but, of course, I won't deny — he is longing for me to go to the Ranch for an extended stay."

"And we are imposing on his good nature, as well as yours, Mother," Moira said apologetically. "You've not been free for a year and a half. You've devoted yourself to Karyn and now Christian. Come on, Karyn darling, make up your mind to come to Rocky and me."

Feeling the stirrings of guilt over her

grandmother, Karyn said, "Give me a little longer, Mother — then I promise you I'll come to Washington." She left the living-room and went to lie down.

Alone with Moira, Joan murmured, "What worries me about Karyn and the others is their complete apathy, and their inability to fight their grief. And there's Claudine, she's leaning more and more on drugs — it's bound to ruin her mind, eventually."

"But, when do Carl and Nicky go back to Harvard?"

"They simply can't decide *that* or anything else. I make suggestions to them — that Karyn should resume ballet lessons, that Claudine prepare to enter Vassar — but it's all useless." She shrugged and broke off as the front door bell rang, Moira went to an-swer it and as she opened the door Nicky, Claudine and Carl burst in.

"Sorry to barge in like this," Nicky spoke quickly, obviously agitated.

One glance at their distressed-looking faces and Joan cried, "Whatever is the mat-ter?"

"Plenty! My parents are starting a legal action over Christian!" Nicky spat the words out.

"We've had the most God-darn stand-up fight with them," Claudine indignantly told

Joan and Moira, "but they've already made a date to see the lawyers. They're wild to get their hands on Christian."

Joan forced herself to be calm, whilst her brain raced. "Sit down and talk this over quietly."

They had settled down when Moira burst out, "Your parents will lose! My husband is one of the finest legal brains in the country."

"Yeah, we told them that," Claudine said, "but Father insists that Nicky appeal against the Puerto Rican divorce decree and claim Christian."

Nicky combed his fingers frantically through his thick golden hair. "I'm moving out — so they can't hammer at me — so is Claudine. Say, Mrs Clements, I need a brandy."

"We *all* do," Joan nodded, "you or Carl please pour it. Now we must *think, think, think!* What's the best thing to do?" an idea was taking hold in her turbulent mind.

"Let me 'phone Rocky, have him fly in! He'll handle everything." Moira jumped up, but Joan waved her back to her chair.

"No, no, wait! God has just given me a marvellous idea." She fixed her compelling eyes on Nicky, then Claudine. "Neither of you want to stay at home — is that right? You *really* want to leave?"

"You've said it!" Nicky nodded, and Claudine cried, "I'm over age and I'm quitting that heap of Stately Stone and Brick."

"You, Carl — you don't want to return to Harvard yet — do you?" Joan sounded like an inquisitor.

"No, I want to hang around with Claudine and the others."

"Right! Then I've got the answer to all the problems — the way to win this little private war over Christian. You must all leave the country at once!"

"Oh Grans!" Karyn wailed, as she came in from the bedroom. "I've heard everything! I'll be lost if they leave me, especially if a lawsuit . . ."

"They *won't* leave you!" Joan said, triumphantly. "They'll take you and Christian with them. Not even all the Van Buren money will tempt a lawyer to be crazy enough to start a custody suit for Christian when the child is with his mother, and with his . . ." She stopped for a second, then very deliberately spelled out, "F–A–T–H–E–R and, don't forget, that's how Christian's Birth Certificate reads — the father is Nicholas Van Buren."

"Mother!" Moira cried, "It's a brilliant plan — a marvellous solution."

Nicky jumped up, waving his brandy glass

on high, "Christ, yes! I go for it!" Claudine broke into hysterical laughter, "That will outwit them all!"

"It sure will!" Carl tossed his brandy down. "But, where do we make for?"

"The world is your oyster!" Moira waved around, expansively.

"But some place off the beaten track," Karyn said, as the weight in her heart lightened a little.

"Yeah, how about a Greek Island?" Nicky's eyes were alight with enthusiasm. "When we were kids, Roy and I figured on one day spending some time on one of them — you know, sleeping out under the stars, catching fish ourselves for breakfast."

That was all the others needed to make them decide that Greece was their location.

"Okay then, what about Hydra?" Carl glanced eagerly around at the others. "My mother went there as a girl — she was crazy about it, she says. It can't have changed much — I guess we fly to Athens and latch onto a boat that runs to the islands."

"Let's book your flight to Athens *now!*" Moira suggested anxious to avoid a change of heart in the four of them.

"Yeah! I'll buy that, I'm all for lamming out of here fast as we can," Nicky said. "Claudine and I can sneak home and grab our passports without being seen. We won't stop for clothes, we'll buy what we need."

"Sure, we'll pick things up in Hydra." Claudine smiled for the first time since Roy's death, "Okay kids, let's go get the 'plane tickets."

Twenty-six

What Joan enjoyed most about life on the ranch were the early mornings when, after breakfast, she and David sat on the porch talking about a thousand different things. There was so much to say to each other, to catch up on the years that had divided them.

Now she sat staring out over the vast expanse of greenery rolling on to join the skyline. David's tall figure, in faded blue cotton pants and shirt, came slowly from the mail box where the mail van deposited letters.

"Two letters for you, darling!" David waved them over his head. "From Greece — I know that pleases you."

"Oh, how right you are." She jumped up to meet him at the top of the steps. "From Karyn." She started to slit the envelope open. "Do you want to hear it?"

"You bet I do." He settled in his chair then tamped tobacco into the bowl of his pipe, as Joan's eyes skimmed over the address, Kala Ligardia, Hydra, Greece. Then she began to read aloud.

Darling Grans,

Hope you and D.D. are well and happy. Please forgive me for not having written for a couple of weeks, but I am busy from morning until night. We are still mad about 'our' island which, as I've told you, is not beautiful in the ordinary way, but the flat-roofed white-washed houses, surrounded by bushes of sweet-smelling herbs and olive trees make a super picture.

We have stuck to our first programme, up at 5.30 A.M., Nicky and Carl go to the beach to buy fish out of the nets being dragged in, then Claudine and I cook them. Afterwards, we swim in the purple-blue sea, an unbelievable colour. Christian is marvellous and, when Nicky holds him around the waist in the sea, he splashes about like a strong swimmer.

Nicky is studying classical Greek with the monks in an ancient monastery on the hill. He says he prefers it to reading Law at Harvard, and intends to be a Greek professor. Carl helps the local Doctor in the little hospital, and learns a lot from seeing medicine in practice.

Thank God, Claudine is entirely off dope. Isn't that great? She helps an old

English spinster who runs a little school for small children and loves it. My time is taken up with my angelic little son who is crawling everywhere, and into everything.

What we are mad about is the simplicity of the life. No honking car horns, no screeching brakes, instead our sounds are monastery bells floating down the hills, and goats' bells drifting on the early morning and evening air.

For some time now, we have been able to talk of our beloved Roy without feeling we are bleeding to death. As you know, Nicky is wild about Christian, and it's a strange sensation for me when Nicky rides Christian on his shoulders, with Chris' legs around Nicky's neck, and I look at them — so alike, with their golden hair and two pairs of blue-blue eyes so like Roy's. I feel Roy — his spirit, maybe — is happy whenever we are all together.

Oh, I forgot the most important news — Claudine and Carl are getting married in two weeks, at the monastery. Isn't that great? We're having a party for our island friends. I *wish* you and D.D. could be here, darling Grans but, maybe you'll visit us one of these days.

All my love, also to D.D. God bless you.

Affectionately,
Karyn

P.S. Could you send this letter on to Mother? Glad to know she is happy in Washington.

Joan looked over at David, and spoke tenderly, "It's so good to hear that they have recovered from their terrible tragedy. They had a gruelling time — it was worse than an ordinary death."

"They sound happy — all right. I guess, after a couple of years of the simple life, the boys will return to Harvard. But, time off won't hurt them, they're so young. Who's the other letter from?"

"Claudine. I'll read it to you."

Hi Mrs Clements,

I should have written light-years ago to say 'thanks a million' for everything. It is really you who made us come here, and the life is swell for us.

Confidentially — Nicky is wild about Karyn and wants to marry her. I've begged her to make it a double wedding with Carl and me, but she says it's too soon after Roy's death.

I tell her that's nuts because, although darling Roy died six months ago, he really left us eighteen months ago. Above all, Nicky and Karyn — I reckon — are falling in love. Not like she was with Roy I guess but, if she married Nicky her love would surely grow. He is such a swell guy, and I've a hunch Roy *wants* them to marry.

Anyhow, that's it. I guess you can't do much from where you are, but I sure wish you were here to make Karyn see the light.

Love to you and D.D.

Affectionately,

Claudine

Happiness surged through Joan. At last! — this was the news she had been longing for. Karyn, safe and happy as Nicky's wife. She folded the letter and looked up into David's face. "Well, darling, what a wonderful thing that Karyn's life will come right once more — thank God."

"And, thank you! I know my love, it's just what you *intended* to happen — you lovely, innocent-looking matchmaker. Marriage would be, of course, the answer for Nicky, Karyn and Christian."

"Of course it's the answer! Oh Lord, if only I could talk to Karyn, but they've no 'phone at their cottage."

"Forget the 'phone! I'll take you to Hydra. How about that?"

"David darling!" She jumped up and rushed to throw her arms around him, smiling up at him with wide joy-filled eyes. "That's marvellous! How soon can we arrive there?"

"Hold everything," he laughed happily. "I've got to 'phone San Francisco Airport to see if they have a flight to Athens, or a good connection in New York, perhaps. How soon can you be ready?"

"At once!" She threw her head back, laughing up at him. "No, in an hour — even less. Oh how I *love* you — *love* you!"

"Darling, although I can't give you a wedding ring yet — by God I will do everything else on earth to make you happy."

"David," she whispered through swiftly arisen sobs, "with . . . you . . . I'm happier . . . than I have ever . . . been."

In her heart she sang a joyous hallelujah to God for his great goodness to Karyn, Moira and herself.

We hope you have enjoyed this Large Print book. Other Thorndike Press or Chivers Press Large Print books are available at your library or directly from the publishers.

For more information about current and upcoming titles, please call or write, without obligation, to:

Thorndike Press
P.O. Box 159
Thorndike, Maine 04986 USA
Tel. (800) 223-2336

OR

Chivers Press Limited
Windsor Bridge Road
Bath BA2 3AX
England
Tel. (0225) 335336

All our Large Print titles are designed for easy reading, and all our books are made to last.